## ABOUT THE AUTHOR

DICK KING-SMITH needs no introduction
as the bestselling, award-winning author, famous
for *Harriet's Hare*, *The Guard Dog*, *The Sheep-Pig* (a
box-office hit when released as the film *Babe*), and
many more. Voted Children's Author of the Year in
1992, and winner of the Children's Book Award in
1995, Dick King-Smith has opened up new ground
with *Godhanger*, which has won him great acclaim as
well as many new readers.

A farmer for many years, Dick King-Smith is now a
full-time author, living and working in a 17th century
cottage near Bristol.

## ABOUT THE ARTIST

ANDREW DAVIDSON trained as a designer at
the Royal College of Art before becoming an
illustrator. His beautiful, distinctive wood engravings
are cut on English boxwood blocks. In 1986 he won
the D&AD Silver Award and the Emil/Kurt Maschler
Award for his illustrations for *The Iron Man* by Ted
Hughes. His artwork for *Godhanger* won the
inaugural children's book prize in **Images 22** – *the best
of British Illustration*, an annual competition run by the
Association of Illustrators. He lives in Gloucestershire
with his wife and two small sons

All Transworld titles are available by post from:

**Book post, PO Box 29,
Douglas, Isle of Man IM99 1BQ**

Credit cards accepted.
Please telephone 01624 836000, fax 01624 837033
Internet http://www.bookpost.co.uk or e-mail:
bookshop@enterprise.net for details.

**Free postage and packing in the UK.**
Overseas customers: allow £1 per book (paperbacks) and
£3 per book (hardbacks).

'A wonderful examination of sacrifice and redemption, a rich tale packed with character and incident that grows from Dick King-Smith's deep knowledge of animals, but which is darker than anything he has done before. This is almost a case of Dick King-Smith meets Ted Hughes, with a dash of D.H. Lawrence in blood-sacrifice mode for good measure ... A marvellous compelling story which repays careful reading, and will become a classic' *Daily Telegraph*

'Beautifully illustrated ... The reader is left with greater knowledge of nature as well as the satisfaction of a really good read' *1015 Magazine, The Times*

'Unflinching realism with a poetic, often sensual lyricism ... A darkly atmospheric thriller with a cast of murderous wild animals ... the rich dark feel of the descriptive writing is magnificently reflected in the linear rhythms and velvety, crepuscular tones of Andrew Davidson's wood engravings' *The Guardian*

'Superbly written and serious in tone, this is an extraordinarily moving story for older juniors' *Junior Education*

'A finely crafted book, carefully written, revelling in description and imagery ... For his insights into nature and his vivid descriptions of them, Dick King-Smith is an exceptional writer. In the new, more sober voice of Godhanger, he shows just what a good storyteller and writer he is' *Julia Eccleshare, Books for Keeps*

# GODHANGER
# Dick King-Smith

*illustrated by*
**Andrew Davidson**

CORGI BOOKS

GODHANGER
A CORGI BOOK: 0 552 545015

First published in Great Britain by Doubleday,
a division of Transworld Publishers Ltd

PRINTING HISTORY
Doubleday edition published 1966
Corgi edition published 1997

3 5 7 9 10 8 6 4

Copyright © Fox Busters Ltd, 1996
Illustrations copyright © Andrew Davidson, 1996

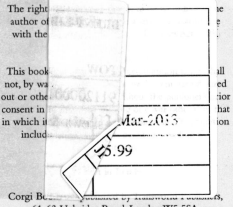

Corgi Books                                    ers,
61–63 Uxbridge Road, London W5 5SA,
a division of The Random House Group Ltd,
in Australia by Random House Australia (Pty) Ltd,
20 Alfred Street, Milsons Point, Sydney, NSW 2016, Australia,
in New Zealand by Random House New Zealand Ltd,
18 Poland Road, Glenfield, Auckland 10, New Zealand
and in South Africa by Random House (Pty) Ltd,
Endulini, 5a Jubilee Road, Parktown 2193, South Africa.

Made and printed in Great Britain by
Mackays of Chatham PLC, Chatham, Kent

# GODHANGER

## CHAPTER ONE

Three hundred metres below, Godhanger Wood lay still in evening sunshine. Gliding silently across the darkening sky, his flight feathers spread like fingertips, Loftus the raven looked down at the massed treetops, the green of their myriad leaves now changing to the reds, golds and browns of autumn.

The shape of the wood was plain to him, lying along the slope of a valley or combe. In outline it resembled the head and neck of a horse. There was even a clearing at just the place to give an impression of an eye.

In the shelter of the hill, the hardwood trees – oak, beech, ash, sycamore and chestnut – grew for the most part straight and skyward, but at the ridge, along the horse's neck, only a hog-mane of thorn and hedge-maple survived, bent crookback by the fierce sea-winds.

The breeze on which Loftus rode came also

from the west, a light air, a breath only, and his all-seeing eyes marked how motionless was the canopy of Godhanger Wood. The only movement below him was that of another bird, almost as large as himself but dark brown instead of his glossy sable, that wheeled endlessly above the valley bottom on broad unmoving wings. Buzzard-baiting appealed to Loftus' sense of humour, and he tipped off his pitch and fell like a black arrow towards the big hawk.

'Whee-oo!' cried the bird in distress at the sound of the raven's coming, and threw himself sideways in frantic flapping haste. Again, 'Whee-oo!' mewed the buzzard, as Loftus shot past him, and his plaintive cries were echoed by his mate, hunting behind the hill.

'Pee-oo! Pee-oo!' called the hen bird in reply, and they said to each other, 'It's that damned raven again.' 'I suppose he thinks it's amusing.'

At that moment they saw Loftus come swooping up over the top of the hill, and, still complaining, they made their heavy way off in search of more peaceful hunting grounds.

Chuckling in his deep voice, the raven climbed above the wood, circling as he gained height, and watching the treetops darkening as the daylight died.

Now his old familiar nesting-place beckoned, high on a sheltered ledge on the Atlantic cliffs, with his old familiar mate, mother in her time to his many children; the gruff-spoken, hairy-chinned, comfortable roosting partner at the end of so many thousands of days. He was just about to turn for home when he saw a solitary black and white bird flying silently along the wood's edge. As he watched, it perched for a moment in the top of a single outlying skeleton-elm, long tail dipping up and down, and then flew suddenly and rapidly away with loud calls of alarm.

'Chakka-chakka-chakka-chak!' cried Myles the magpie, and Loftus circled higher still. He knew Myles for a thief and a double-dyed villain, but he also knew better than to doubt the 'pie's warning.

And at that precise moment the evening's peace was shattered by the blast of a gunshot. After a heartbeat's pause came the noise of a second shot, followed by a thin agonized screaming that ceased as suddenly as it had arisen. Silence fell again on Godhanger Wood as the raven beat away towards the west.

★ ★ ★

The two spent cartridges spun away as the game-keeper broke open his gun. He reloaded and stood still, eyes narrowed, watching his dog working a bramble-patch. Very soon she came running to the man, a squealing rabbit in her mouth, and laid it, broken-legged and bulging-eyed, before him. The noise stopped abruptly as the game-keeper took the rabbit and broke its neck.

One glance at the limp body told him that it was a milky doe, its belly plucked of the soft fur in which now, somewhere, its kittens were warmly snuggled and would soon lie cold and stiff.

Gun in the crook of his left arm, he pulled from his right-hand coat pocket a bone-handled knife and opened its ten-centimetre blade. Neatly he slashed the middle of the doe's upturned belly between the two rows of swollen teats, closed and replaced the knife, then reached in and twisted out guts and paunch, which he tossed away into the undergrowth.

The dog made no move but sat watching, hoping, on this occasion rightly, that the carcase would be hers at the end of the day. The game-keeper slipped the rabbit into his game-bag and wiped his red hand on the silky hair of the spaniel's back. Then he straightened up and set off again, dog at heel, with long strides through the tall trees of Godhanger.

All was quiet as before his coming, all was as it had been, save for two orange-coloured cartridge cases on the ground, and, caught upon a bramble, a little festoon of warm innards whose coils still wriggled and slid uneasily.

A meat-fly landed upon the guts, and stood, moving its feet in pleased anticipation until it was dislodged by a final spasmodic motion of the glazing intestines. They slipped from the briar and fell to the ground.

After a gap of time the stillness of the darkening wood was broken. At intervals, among the great oaks and beeches, there were a few small stands of larches, and into these, homecoming pigeons began to crash. Nearer, a pair of little owls started up their shrill, plaintive cries. Above the bramble-patch, on a low bough of a big horse chestnut, a robin sang with that heart-catching wistfulness that tells of summer gone and hard cold nights to come. The breeze had dropped to nothing. Nothing moved.

Suddenly, quite silently, a head appeared, poking out beneath the tangle of blackberry bushes. It was a blackish head with white marks about the sharp muzzle and between eye and ear.

For a moment the head moved to and fro, quick, questing nostrils dilated to suck in the gut-scent – and then, out of the briar patch slid the low, dark, humpbacked shape of Rippin the polecat, foul-smelling killer of any creature that might come his way. Unlike other animals, it was the nature of his kind to kill and keep on killing. He was programmed to do so. Mice, rats, ground-nesting birds, frogs, snakes – all were fair game to Rippin, as indeed was far larger prey when chance offered: in his time he had put paid to many chickens, and once, one glorious, never-to-be-forgotten winter's night, sixteen turkeys had died to satisfy his blood-lust. Such monsters, of course, he had not been able to drag away, but they had provided a feast of his favourite delicacy: the brains.

However, Rippin was not fussy. Rabbit guts would do for starters. He had begun to tug and gulp at them, growling softly in his throat, when suddenly, from out of nowhere, a broad-winged shape came swooping noiselessly upon him with talons hanging ready to grasp, only to sheer away at the last moment as the polecat rose up on his hind legs to his full height, all forty-five centimetres of it, his mouth agape, his coarse fur on end, and chattered in fearless fury.

'Damn you! Damn you!' he raved, dancing in his rage. 'If I could only catch hold of you, I'd have the feathers off you, I'd tear your throat out, suck your blood, chew up your great staring eyeballs, I'd kill you, kill you, kill you!' And the air about grew thick with his choking, acrid stink.

Circling, the tawny owl flew back and pitched on a branch of the chestnut to stare silently down, till at last the polecat ceased his cursing and made off, towing a rope of guts with him and grumbling all the while. 'Bloody owls, I hate 'em, I hate 'em,' the bird could hear, until finally the sound passed beyond even his acute earshot.

'Horrible beast,' said the tawny owl softly to himself. He straightened a feather or two on his streaky breast, and swivelled his round head to look all about him.

'That's the nastiest-natured creature in Godhanger, bar none,' he said. 'Sure as my name is Glyde.'

'Glyde.'

The word was instantly repeated, like an echo. But it was not an echo. The name was spoken in a different voice, a voice whose authority was instantly recognizable, even in the uttering of that monosyllable.

Glyde looked up into the branches high above. 'Master?' he said. 'Is it you?'

From somewhere high within the still-leafy crown of the horse chestnut, a great shape dropped on silent wings, and pitched upon the tawny owl's branch, almost half a metre below him. Even so, their heads were on a level. This was the mighty bird who had come to Godhanger Wood, known to those that lived there as the Skymaster.

Some of the birds of the wood had come together as followers of the Skymaster, and all these carried different pictures of him in their minds. Because all found themselves unable to meet his gaze directly, each tended to think of him in the image of his own kind, as some sort of hawk or falcon or crow or owl. Only once in their lives were they able to look directly at him, and then it was too late.

Glyde looked away as usual, saying, 'You called, Master?'

Had he been able to see the other's eyes, he would have noticed a twinkle in them. ' "The nastiest-natured creature in Godhanger" I think you remarked?' said the Skymaster. His tone was not of rebuke but of amusement. 'Why so, my friend?'

'He is evil-tempered,' said Glyde.

'He was angry, yes, certainly. But there are times when anger rouses each and every one of us.'

'Not you, Master.'

'That you have not known me angered does not mean, Glyde, that I have never been so, or that you will never so see me. Anger may be healthy, cleansing, a relief to the spirit at certain times, just as a violent thunderstorm clears the air and cools the overheated land.'

The tawny owl scratched the side of his round face with a claw. 'At certain times, maybe,' he said reasonably. 'But Rippin the foumart is always angry.' He used the old name for a polecat, the marten that is foul-scented, though the word itself was meaningless to him, since like almost all the birds, he had little or no sense of smell.

'And,' he went on, 'he is always hungry for the taste of blood.'

'Do you not kill?' asked the Skymaster.

'Yes, but for food, not for fun, Master. To feed myself, my mate, our owlets. To this end the roosting bird must die, the rat, the mouse, the cockchafer. I cannot live by berries alone. It is not in my nature.'

'Yet your nature – for this is what you are saying – is less nasty than the polecat's? You are a nicer creature (remembering that just now it was you who dived upon him), you are more to be esteemed, of greater value, more likeable?'

'Yes, Master,' said Glyde stubbornly. 'I think I am.'

'Perhaps then,' said the Skymaster, 'you had better try to think better of Rippin the polecat, lest you too become nasty-natured, as you say he is,' and he spread his great wings and sailed away into the darkness.

The tawny owl sat for some minutes and bent his head to peer at the ground below. The moonlight glinted upon the brass ends of two cartridge cases that lay in the short grass of the floor of the wood, and Glyde put his head on one side to consider better this unusual pair of shining eyes.

His was not the only curious gaze, for in a moment there came the tiniest scratching noise to tense his muscles, and a woodmouse appeared from its hole between the tree roots and began a series of little darting runs towards the strange objects. Instantly Glyde dropped like a stone from his branch to take the mouse in one foot. The four curved talons crushed out its life, and into

Glyde's beak it went headfirst, the tail sticking out just for a second, waving a little as though the woodmouse were still alive.

Then from deeper in the wood there came the noise of grunting, and the tawny owl gulped down his meal and flew silently away.

Now the grunting sounds grew louder, and presently there emerged into a moonlit clearing a low, heavy animal that walked flat-footed with the slow rolling shuffle of a bear, stopping often for a scratch or to nose about for food.

Baldwin the badger was the least fussy of feeders. Anything that was edible he ate – fledgling birds fallen from the nest, mice, voles, hedgehogs even, plus insects, especially the larvae of wasp and bumble-bee, and quantities of earthworms.

'Snakes', he would say, 'are very tasty. I'm very partial to a nice grass-snake. But what I really relish is a nest of young rabbits. Delicious, they are.'

Never a fast mover, even as a young boar, Baldwin in old age took life very steadily. Let the junior badgers go galloping about Godhanger, burning up their energy in play, or mating, or fighting. He was past all that, he told himself. A solitary badger now, he told himself everything, finding comfort in this, as the old often do.

'Always look after Number One, Baldwin, my boy,' he would say. 'You're not so sprack as you were, and the old bones ache a bit when the wind's in the north. So long as you can keep the old belly full, that's what matters. Still got your teeth, praise be. And your nose.'

Now, as Baldwin reached the bramble-patch beneath the horse chestnut, that nose brought him a sudden clear message.

'Hullo, hullo!' he said. 'I smell rabbit,' and he poked his white-striped head into the under-growth and sniffed deeply.

The doe whose guts Rippin had eaten had been a stub-rabbit, a rabbit that contrives to live its life not in tunnels below ground but in runs beneath heather or furze bushes or, as here, within a tangle of briars.

Nothing now remained of the doe but her pelt, flung on the midden behind the game-keeper's cottage, for his spaniel had gone to her kennel full-fed. But her five kittens still stirred feebly in the shallow scrape which she had dug for this late and last litter under the blackberry bushes.

Baldwin pushed his twenty-kilo frame into

the briar fortress, his thick silvery coat armouring him against the spears and lances of the defending thorns, and dug out and ate the five babies in less than half that number of minutes. Then, clucking with pleasure, he made his rolling way to the horse chestnut's nearest neighbour, a giant grey-skinned beech tree, one of several within the wood that he used to clean and sharpen his claws upon. Its smooth bark was scored vertically to a height of a metre or more by the marks of his many visits, and he stood against the trunk and added to their number.

'That's better, Baldwin, my dear,' said Baldwin, dropping back on all fours and giving himself a good shake. 'That's a good start. And the night's still young so stir your stumps and let's be off again,' and he trundled away through the trees.

Above him, in those trees, many of the animals of Godhanger Wood perched or sat or lay. Some were creatures of the night as he was, and heard or watched his passing as he rustled through the first-fallen leaves. Some were of the daytime and paid no heed to the badger, but slept sound and waited for the dawn.

There were birds in plenty, but there were beasts aloft too. There were bats in those trees that age or disease or lightning had hollowed, squirrels snug in their bulky dreys, and in his nest in the low crown of an ancient thickset oak there crouched a fearsome figure that peered down with eyes of coldest green at Baldwin as he snuffled noisily among the roots below, and showed its fangs in a soundless snarl. This was Gilbert the wild cat.

Everything about Gilbert was twisted: his corkscrew tail (caught and broken in a gin-trap), his beat-up ears, his nature. Chance survivor of a litter of farm kittens murdered by a roving cannibal tom, he viewed the world through a haze of bitterness. He had no friends amongst the woodlanders, from the smallest to the largest, from the pygmy shrew who weighed five grams to the thirty-kilo roe buck. He especially hated any invasion of his territory. Mateless, childless, friendless, Gilbert's home was all in all to him. No matter that it was only a rough hollow four metres up in the ruined oak, it was his den, and so, to his way of thinking, the tree was his and he cursed all who came near it.

Now he began to growl deep in his throat at the badger rootling below.

'Temper, temper!' cried a cheerful voice above him, and, peering up, the wild cat saw a small tubby shape perched on a branch directly over his head. It was a little owl, and at sight of this second intruder, Gilbert positively spat with anger. His green eyes glowed, and his unsheathed claws rasped on the bark at the rim of his hole in impotent fury.

'One of these nights,' he hissed, 'I shall kill you. Slowly.'

The small squat bird, whose name was Eustace, gave a sharp bark of amusement.

'First catch your owl,' he said, and then by way of comment opened wide his gape and brought up a pellet composed of mouse skin, bones and beetle fragments. The pellet narrowly missed Gilbert's head and fell to earth in front of Baldwin, who swallowed it absently before lumbering away in search of more appetizing food.

'That's more like it!' said Eustace comfortably. 'I bet you wish you could do that, old moggy. It must be very unpleasant having to digest all the rubbish you eat. Probably what makes you so bad-tempered.'

'I hate you,' said Gilbert softly.

'That's your trouble, old moggy,' said Eustace. 'You hate everybody. You should try listening to someone I know.'

'Who might that be?'

'He is known as the Skymaster. He is the greatest of birds.'

'A bird! I should listen to a bird!'

'He is not like other birds,' said Eustace.

All the time that they had been talking, Gilbert, infinitely slowly, was altering his position, inching forward from the mouth of his hole, setting his hind feet and gradually twisting his body, ready for a sudden upward pounce that would carry him the short distance to the little owl's perch, but a split second before he sprang, Eustace jumped nimbly off his branch. Striking and missing, Gilbert lost his footing and tumbled and slid all anyhow down the trunk of the oak, spitting and snarling with rage.

'Love your enemies!' shouted Eustace. 'Do good to those that hate you, old moggy!' and he swooped away, quick and low, with a final burst of laughter.

## CHAPTER TWO

O f those who had fallen under the spell of the Skymaster as they listened to his words and strove to understand his teachings, Eustace was the odd bird out.

Though, like them, he thought of himself as a follower of the great strange bird that had come to Godhanger, he was not quite as wholehearted as the rest. Something in his nature would not allow him to trust so blindly, so single-mindedly, in the words of the Master. It was not exactly cynicism, more a kind of scepticism.

Eustace did believe that here was an animal of extraordinary powers, but he could not find it in himself to treat the Skymaster as a supernatural being in the way that, for instance, his larger cousin Glyde the tawny owl did.

He positively worships him, old Glyde does, Eustace thought. He'd probably lay down his life for him. I don't think I would. Look after

Number One, that's my motto. I managed quite nicely before the Skymaster came, and I expect I still shall after he's gone.

A large moth fluttered by, and the little owl took it neatly in flight and swooped up into a nearby tree to eat it. It appealed to Eustace's sense of humour to conduct a conversation with the late moth, now in his crop.

'Sorry, moth,' he said. 'I'm afraid I've rather spoiled your night out. Presumably I've made some other moth a widow, or a widower – I've no idea what sex you are . . . were, I mean. But I didn't do you in with malice aforethought, old moth, take my word for it. I have no grudge against you, old moth, I do assure you. On the contrary, what I feel for you is love, the love of a tender morsel of moth-meat. I am a great lover of tender morsels, of vole-meat and mouse-meat, of the flesh of little birds and the innards of beetles, and of bite-sized bits of the wriggling worm. All must die to keep Eustace in good nick. And lastly I console you, my lepidopterous friend, with the thought that some day or night Eustace will drop off his perch and be loved in his turn, by the ants and the maggots.'

In the darkness – darkness, that is to say, to humans but not to little owls – another moth came fluttering past, and Eustace took off, snapped it out of the air, returned to his perch, and swallowed it down.

'Neatly done,' he said, addressing this second victim, 'though I say it myself. For all his wonderful powers, I doubt that the Master could have done that, my good moth. Let us hope that, by some quirk of fate, you are the other half of a happy moth-marriage, and are now reunited with your mate. It would be pleasant to think that in death you are not divided,' and crying 'Cu-cu-cu-cu!' in merry appreciation of his own wit, Eustace flew off in search of further prey.

To the eyes of the high flyers, like the pair of buzzards, Loftus the raven, and the slatey-grey peregrine falcons who came in from the sea-cliffs to take pigeons, the horsehead shape of Godhanger far below them had two special features.

One was a building, at the centre or pupil of that little clearing that was the eye of the horse. This was the cottage of the gamekeeper, a place to which almost all the birds gave a wide berth.

The other was a grove of trees at the lowest point of the horse's neck, on the far edge of the wood, where a small stream meandered in the bottom of the combe. These trees were quite distinct from the many native kinds. They were exotic, ornamental trees, impressive not only for their foreignness but for their size. The animals of Godhanger had grown up with them and so never bothered their heads about what hand might have planted this outlandish cluster, many lifetimes ago. But it was nevertheless a special place to them, different from any other part of the wood and not solely on account of the strangeness of the trees.

Whenever they crawled or hopped or walked or flew among those towering sequoias and great dark cone-shaped deodars, those pale waving locust trees and spiky sentinel monkey-puzzles, a feeling came upon each and every bird and beast, a feeling that they could not explain or identify. To be sure, the grove was a part of Godhanger Wood, but it had its own identity, its own peculiar atmosphere. And within it, at its centre, there stood one single tree where all experienced these strange sensations most strongly.

This was a cedar of Lebanon, a giant among its fellows, not so much in height for its huge bole was of no great measure, but by virtue of the spread of its great arms, a spread that began perhaps three metres above the ground. Higher, the trunk divided into many stems, each in its turn throwing out branches, with each branch curving at first a little upwards and then at its end lying almost horizontal, so that a great tract of the floor was overshadowed and barren beneath the tree's broad evergreen umbrella.

Here in the cedar of Lebanon, in the grove in Godhanger, was the home of the Skymaster. Or more accurately, here was the place where he was most likely to be found by those that sought him. Always he sat upon a particular bough. That was his perch, and his alone.

At first light, their established meeting time, the birds would come to the grove, to the cedar of Lebanon, whether at the joyful early rising of the summer sun when all Godhanger rang with the dawn chorus of a thousand throats, or in the dead of winter when the day came late and grey and grudgingly and the cedar's long arms leaped and swayed in the cold sea-winds. This was the chosen hour, the handover time between the creatures of the night and of the day, and always there would be some, even if it were only two or three gathered together, who would find themselves drawn to the cedar tree, to listen, or to question.

Indeed, that very next morning after the death of the milky doe stub-rabbit, while Rawden, the old brown rat who lived in the gamekeeper's midden, was still licking the last shreds of fat from her hide, and while Rippin the polecat in his den and Baldwin the badger deep in his sett were digesting the night's fare to which she had contributed, three of the followers of the Skymaster sat around him in the cedar of Lebanon.

Glyde the tawny owl was there, and the little owl Eustace, and beside them the square-tailed, heavy-billed shape of a carrion crow. A fourth follower, the magpie Myles, sat in the very top of the tree, flirting his long greeny-black tail as he scanned the grove for danger.

It was a still, windless dawn, almost noiseless too, for the choristers sang no longer at this time of the year. The sky was empty, for the swallows and swifts had gone south. The only movement that Myles could see was at the fringe of the grove where it met the home-bred trees. Here, a few first falling leaves seesawed and twirled their way down to earth, to moulder and decay and be dragged underground by the sexton worms to provide nourishment for new leaf-growth in due season.

Satisfied, Myles called down, 'All clear, Master.'

Then, as at each dawn, the Skymaster spoke. 'My friends,' he said. 'May good fortune guide you through the day to come, whether you go to your rest or start about your business. Young or old, swift or slow, strong or weak, hunter or hunted, may you fare well until we meet once more.'

'May it be so!' answered the tawny owl and the carrion crow, whose name was Darcy, and from the treetop, Myles the magpie echoed their words.

Eustace was unable to make the customary response with the others because he was in the act of bringing up a pellet. He voided it quickly, gulped, 'May it be so!' and added 'Master' for luck.

'Oh, Master, Master,' said Glyde in unctuous tones. 'Now that you are come to Godhanger, what harm can come to us?'

'Well, I can think of someone who could do you a bit of mischief,' said Eustace tartly, 'not a couple of minutes' flight from here. With a gun. And a dog. And a long bit of board nailed to a post at the top of his garden, with a long row of dead animals hanging from it. Any time you get to feeling you don't give a hoot about life, Glyde old pal, you just pop down there. You go and have a look at the man's gibbet. Last time I was near enough, I counted six bodies on it. Don't know what they were – could have been anything from stoats or weasels or squirrels to one of us, I wasn't going nearer to find out.'

He swivelled his round head to stare directly at Glyde. 'Harm came to them all right, didn't it?' he said. 'They were dead and hung up to rot. Shot or trapped or poisoned to death. Death. The end for all of us. There's nothing after death.'

'How do you know, little owl of little faith?' said the Skymaster softly.

'Oh dear, oh dear!' said Eustace, bobbing and bowing on his perch in a kind of comic bewilderment. 'I just don't get it.' He swivelled his head to look at his two companions to left and to right. 'Do you?' he said.

'It is hard to believe,' said Darcy.

Somewhat patronizingly, Glyde addressed himself to his smaller cousin. 'It is not easy for you to understand,' he said.

'It is not meant to be easy,' said the Skymaster, 'for anyone.'

A silence fell. The day had strengthened, and the crow began to fidget, anxious to be away in search of food, live or dead. Both the owls were yawning in the growing light.

At that moment they heard a jay scream deeper in the wood, and immediately Myles gave his chattering alarm-call. Wings were spread, muscles tensed, feet thrust down against bark, and the four followers were gone their separate ways. Only the Skymaster sat tall and still in the green gloom of the cedar of Lebanon.

The screaming of the jay continued, its harsh 'Skraak!' becoming louder as it approached the grove. The bird was flying ahead of the gamekeeper, just out of gunshot range, moving from tree to tree with its quick though clumsy-looking action. Each time it pitched, it looked back, raised its black-streaked crest, and shrieked another warning to all the animals in Godhanger. It was a hen bird, and for two days now the corpse of its mate had hung upon the gibbet, the colour faded from the pinkish body and the once brilliant blue barring of wing coverts.

'Murderer!' screeched the widow. 'Heartless murderer! Skraak!'

At the edge of the grove the gamekeeper stopped and stood behind the trunk of a large cypress. He held his gun in his right hand, muzzle upward, barrels resting against his shoulder, and with the palm of his left hand he made a down-ward motion to his dog. The spaniel dropped and lay perfectly still.

The gamekeeper hated jays. Of the many creatures that lived in and about Godhanger (almost all of whom he loathed) he reserved a special degree of hatred for jays. It was not only on account of their liking for pheasant eggs and chicks, for there was no shortage of others with similar tastes. He detested them for their flashi-ness, for their impudence, and above all for their noisiness. Once sighted by a jay, there was no escape from that harsh relentless voice that adver-tised his presence to all. He, most silent of movers, might just as well walk through the wood beating a drum.

Now, rock-still and infinitely patient, he waited for a chance to trade upon another of the screamer's traits – curiosity. He knew what it would want to know – where was he?

Standing against the cypress trunk, the tall figure of the gamekeeper might almost have been part of the tree. Everything about him was dark – the black of his boots and his gun barrels, the swarthiness of hands and what little of his face could be seen beneath a shapeless olive-coloured hat pulled well down, the indescribable murkiness of the long, deep-pocketed coat he wore – a dull dark brown, a dull dark green, a dull dark grey; it was all of those.

Nothing of him was bright or pale except his eyes. Beneath the rim of the hat, they were a brilliant icicle-blue. Beneath the eyes, the shadowy countenance was a wreck of sharp angles and hollows and deep-cut lines. Just as the facade of a ruined castle is somehow more compelling than its original state can ever have been, so the face of the gamekeeper drew the gaze – for those, that is, who lived for a look. Most died without that privilege, in the jaws of a trap, in a wire noose, in a hail of shot: but those that lingered long enough for their necks to need pulling were afforded a glimpse of a long, curved nose a little bent at its bridge, of coppery cheeks seamed with scars and wrinkles like old leather, and of a jaw that jutted so far that the thin, colourless upper lip could not close upon its fellow but lay always behind it in a sneer that was half snarl. Always, to look upon that face was to die.

Now, as he waited, only the eyes of the gamekeeper moved, flicking suddenly from side to side as he heard the jaybird once more. By this time she was in the cedar of Lebanon, jumping rather heavily from one flat spreading bough to another, constantly turning her head to look about. In the absence of anything to see she had ceased for a while to scream, but now began a series of clicking noises. She raised and lowered her fanned-out tail or swung it from side to side.

At last she could bear it no longer. She could see no danger, she could hear no danger, therefore it followed there was no danger. Yet she was curious (as her late husband had been) to know where it had gone. She really must fly back, just a little way, quietly, taking every care, of course. She tensed herself.

'I shouldn't, if I were you,' said a voice.

'Who's that?' cried the hen jay, startled, and then she saw, in the shadowy greenness above her, a large dark shape.

'Oh, it's you,' she said sharply. 'Skymaster or whatever they call you. I'll thank you to mind your own affairs.'

'Your affairs are my affairs,' said the Skymaster. 'I want to protect you, jaybird, as I would protect any of the creatures of Godhanger Wood. Believe in me. I would not fly back that way if I were you.'

'Well, you're not me,' said the jay, 'and I can look after myself, thanks very much.'

'As your mate could?' asked the Skymaster softly.

'How d'you know about that? – oh, you've been down there gawping, I suppose. Or perhaps you expect me to believe what that stupid tawny owl and his friends are always saying – that you see things that are hidden from them and do things that they can't explain; work bloody miracles in fact. Oh, I've heard 'em, droning on in that sickly tone they use when they're discussing you. I'm sick and tired of hearing about you and your precious wisdom and I'm not alone either; there are plenty of woodlanders who feel the same. It's Skymaster this and Skymaster that, gets on my nerves, it does. A load of bloody rubbish, I call it!' cried the jay, and with a final shriek, she set off back towards the cypress tree.

Afterwards she could never precisely recall what happened next. She remembered approaching the cypress, confident that by now there was no danger, and then suddenly, as she neared it, seeing a branch poking out from behind its trunk, a branch that was not a branch because it was too straight and because it was moving and foreshortening until it pointed directly at her.

And then suddenly the jay heard behind her the whistle of wings, and a great shape flashed by and dived at speed, to wheel around the trunk of the cypress. And all at once the branch jerked wildly and exploded in a roar of sound while at the same instant a hail of shot hissed over her head. Simultaneously she saw, even as she braked to turn away, a shapeless olive-coloured hat go flying through the air. Beating madly away to safety, she heard behind her the cursing voice of the man and the yapping of the dog. Then came the crash of a second shot, and then silence.

## CHAPTER THREE

Darcy the carrion crow heard the two gun-shots and looked intently up towards his mate. She was standing sentry in the topmost branches of a walnut tree near the cottage, as she had been since just after the gamekeeper set out.

Each morning it was the habit of the pair of crows, once the enemy was gone, to investigate the gibbet, one keeping watch while the other checked the board for fresh corpses which might provide a tasty breakfast snack. At a pinch – say in the depths of a hard winter – they were not choosy, making do if needs be with the leathery cadavers of the long-dead, but they preferred juicier titbits.

Darcy was now considering setting about the body of the cock jay, but he was taking his time, being a firm believer in the credo of 'Better safe than sorry'. Close acquaintance with the gibbet had given him no desire to end his days there, and he suspected that, though ill-luck might play a part, it was, in the main, foolishness that brought about the downfall of those that hung there and suffered no longer.

The jay that was just too curious, the stoat that turned for a last chatter of defiance, the fox that did not notice the loop of wire, the kestrel that hovered too long – they were fools and so had paid the price.

So when he saw his mate lift away – silently, for she knew he would be watching – he left the gibbet and followed. Together they cleared the upper western edge of the wood, crossed the mane on the ridge, and floated down over the intervening fields towards the sea, speculating companionably in their harsh voices as to what choice carcases the tide might have brought in.

All around, the birds of the air were at work in the bright cold morning, watching and waiting for food, alive or dead. The two buzzards, eaters of carrion as the crows were, hung at their pitches, circling slowly and occasionally mewing plaintively to one another. Kestrels quartered the grasslands and sparrow hawks hunted the hedges, while at the land's edge a thousand gulls swung and clamoured, riding effortlessly on the vertical column of wind that ran up the face of the cliffs.

Sitting at his nest-site, a ledge just below the cliff top, under an overhang of rock, Loftus the raven watched and saw everything, on land, on the sea, in the air. He saw the lollop of the hare grazing in the meadow, he noted the shiny black heave and dip of the surfacing porpoise, he caught the blue lightning flash that was the peregrine falcon, stooping at its prey at a hundred miles an hour. He looked and observed and noted and thought, with all the wisdom of his years, which were very many.

Some creatures, like the mayfly on the stream below Godhanger, had in their season only a day of life; many of the smaller birds were lucky to survive a couple of years; even Baldwin was a very old badger in the tenth autumn of his life. But there was none to compare with Loftus, for he was of a great age.

Since his hatching in a rough nest of sticks, lined with sheep's wool and decorated with hay, seaweed, horsehair and cow-ribs, seventy-five years had come and gone, years in which he had done a great deal of thinking on a wide variety of subjects. Just now, noting the flight to the shore of Darcy and his mate from the ridge behind which lay Godhanger, he was thinking of the wood and its inhabitants, and then of one in particular, the most mysterious. He was thinking about the Skymaster.

Loftus was not a woodland bird. Not more than half a dozen times in all his years had he set foot in Godhanger, whose denseness made him most uneasy the moment he dropped below tree-top level. He was above all a bird of the upper air, together with the peregrines and, in summer, the high-flying swifts, and the gulls that rose spread-winged on the thermals, circling up and up to the limits of sight. There, or in the remoteness of his cliff ledge, he was the master of his fate, safe from the only enemy. But down in Godhanger Wood lived death, and only in bitter times had he ever dared drop in among the trees in search of something to fill his empty crop. The wood, he knew, held a man with a gun, and the voice of the gun was the voice of doom.

There were many creatures, he realized, less fortunate than himself, who must needs dwell in Godhanger to get their livelihood, but who would live there unless he must? This Skymaster, of whom he had heard much – why should he choose to live there? He was a huge bird, Loftus knew by report, strong and swift, and possessed, they said, of strange powers, who had suddenly appeared one winter's day and since then had never left the confines of the wood. Why not? Was he a fool, courting death? Yet all spoke of his wisdom, sat at his feet, apparently, to listen to his words.

Loftus had never heard the Skymaster speak, indeed had never set eyes upon him, but he remembered when first he had heard his name, in a conversation he had once had with the buzzards. As a rule the raven had no time for these birds, considering them to be whining cowards despite their size, and he only used them as butts for bullying. It was fun to dive at the big clumsy hawks, rolling and corkscrewing among them with honks of amusement, and practising his favourite trick of swinging over on to his back and stabbing upwards at them with his big black beak as they cried 'Whee-oo!' in their distress.

But on this particular occasion, he had found them on the ground, in a field on the eastern grassy slope of the combe, opposite Godhanger. They were tugging at a rabbit carcase, and, intent upon their work, did not notice the raven land and hop towards them.

'Krok! Krok!' cried Loftus in his deep voice, and with each call, his whole body lunged forward and the pointed feathers on his throat stood out like a ragged beard. 'Out of my way, you two.'

Mewling, the buzzards flapped heavily up and settled on adjoining posts of the nearby fence.

'It's not fair!' moaned the hen bird. 'Why should he steal our food? Why must we sit here meekly and watch?'

'Because we are cowards,' said the male buzzard. 'We cannot all be brave and strong as the Master is.'

'Tell me more,' said Loftus, with his mouth full and his eyes twinkling. 'Tell me more of this Master of yours, you silly buzzards. Is he of your tribe?'

'Some say he is like a hawk,' said the male bird. 'Yet he is greater than any hawk.'

'Some say he is like a falcon,' said the hen. 'Yet he is swifter than any falcon.'

'Some say he is like an owl,' said the male. 'Yet he is wiser than any owl.'

'You don't sound very sure about the looks of this paragon,' said Loftus drily, wiping his bill on the grass. 'Seems to me you've never studied him properly.'

The buzzards shifted awkwardly on their posts.

'It isn't easy,' said the male, uneasily.

'His eyes . . .' said his mate, blinking her own.

'. . . are terrible,' finished the male buzzard with a shudder.

'You cannot look into them. No one can,' they both said.

What nonsense, Loftus had thought at the time. They're a pack of poltroons, scared of their own shadows.

'I've never met a bird I couldn't look in the eye,' he had said, and, turning his back on the hawks, had fallen to tearing once again at the rabbit.

But now, months later, he was thinking that the matter had never been put to the test. This Skymaster creature remained within the wood, and so they would probably never meet. Yet strangely, on this particular morning, he suddenly felt an undeniable urge to go to Godhanger, and he jumped off his rock-ledge and set off for the ridge behind which the wood lay, a mile distant as the raven flies.

As he came over the top of the hill, something told him to turn south, and then to follow round the perimeter of the horsehead shape towards the nose. Not only was this part of Godhanger much nearer to the cottage than he would normally have cared to go, but he found himself flying lower than usual, though still instinctively well out of gunshot range, and heading towards one particular tree at the outermost fringe of the wood. Over this tree, a holm oak, he circled, peering down into its evergreen depths, and from them, suddenly, he heard a loud clear voice.

'Loftus,' said the voice. 'Come down.'

Despite himself, the raven shut his wings and dropped to treetop height, a height at which, he knew, a blast of shot could come ripping up out of the greenery to smash into his black breast and still for ever the heart that had beaten for seventy-five years.

But something in that voice told Loftus that he would be perfectly safe, and he planed in among the branches and pitched upon one and looked about him.

'Here I am,' said the voice, just behind him, and he jumped around to see who had spoken.

'I've never met a bird I couldn't look in the eye . . .' The words came clearly to mind, as he lifted his gaze and then dropped it instantly. Try as he would, Loftus could not make himself look a second time.

'How . . . do you know my name?' he said.

'All know of Loftus the raven, surely?' said the Skymaster in such a gentle, innocent tone that

Loftus gave way for an instant to a little wave of pure vanity concerning his great age and his strength and wisdom. Was he not revered by everyone, including, it seemed, this creature before him?

But then the wave ebbed away, and he knew without doubt that his thoughts were as plain to the other as if he had spoken them. 'I'm just an old bullier of buzzards,' he said wryly. 'You knew that too, I'm sure? Just as you knew that I would come, this day, to this tree, to meet with you. Why have you called me?'

'I have need of you, Loftus, of your sharp eye and your strong bill.'

'Why me? Why not one of those who call you "Master"?' said Loftus, and he could not keep a small sneer from his voice.

'A title that you would never use?' said the Skymaster, and made a noise that sounded almost like a chuckle.

'I am my own master. You may have need of me but I have none of you. I have never asked help of anyone.'

'You have indeed been lucky, Loftus. Perhaps someone has been watching over you. Nevertheless I would be grateful for your help,' said the Skymaster quietly, and turned on his perch so that his back was towards the raven.

Loftus' first reaction was one of relief from the stare of those eyes that he knew, though his own look was bent, had been fixed upon him. Then, raising his head, he saw immediately, first that the hang of one wing was not normal but hunched and eccentric, and then that its long, bronze primary feathers were spotted and stained with the dark red of dried blood.

'Aaaah!' croaked Loftus softly. He is but a bird like the rest of us, he thought; as much at the mercy of the man as we are, despite this talk of magic powers.

'What must I do?' he said.

'It is not as bad as it looks,' said the Skymaster, exactly as though he could see each bloodstain as clearly as the raven. 'It is not yet my time to die. But there is shot embedded in the joint of the wing, that I cannot reach to remove.'

He paused, and a note of amusement sounded in his voice as he added, 'I am but a bird like the rest of you.'

Loftus hopped close, and began to probe with his great dagger of a beak. Slowly, cautiously, gently, he explored beneath the feathering until he felt the small round hardnesses of the lead under the surface of the skin at the joint.

'It is buried,' he said. 'I must hurt you.'

'Don't be afraid,' said the Skymaster comfortingly, as though it were the other who must suffer the pain, and he sat motionless and unflinching as Loftus pecked and pecked deep, until he found the shot and drew them out in turn, his bill-tip wet with fresh blood.

Satisfied at last, he drew back. 'How does it feel?' he asked.

For answer the Skymaster began to stretch out the injured wing and then refold it, cautiously at first. Again and again he flexed it, now more strongly, until at last he turned and spread wide both pinions, and held them above the head of the raven, in a kind of benediction.

'Bless you, my friend,' he said. 'I shall be healed. Thank you, Loftus.'

Loftus shook himself. 'I don't understand you,' he said bluntly. 'And I don't understand how you came to be shot. You, the greatest, the swiftest, the wisest, they all say.'

'I was helping a fellow creature. As you have.'

'Why did you?' asked Loftus, and he thought – why did I?

'To protect her,' said the Skymaster, 'as you would protect your mate, your chicks, your family. You see, all the birds and beasts of

Godhanger are my family.'

'And you risked your life for one?'

'Today, for one. One day, for another. At the last, for all. Go now, Loftus. Fly home to your well-loved mate on the high sea-cliffs.'

Thinking, later that day on those sea-cliffs, about all that had been said between them that morning in the holm oak, Loftus the raven remembered much that puzzled him. Not the least strange was the final thing that he had said to the Skymaster.

After his dismissal, as he flapped away out of the branches, he had cried out without thinking three last words.

'Take care, Master!' he had said.

Later that day the wind began to rise, blowing hourly more strongly from the far west of the world, until by evening there was a wild, mad storm of air that whipped white the surface of the sea and lifted the breakers to smash them against the foot of the cliffs in towering clouds of spray. The force of the gale ran up the cliff-face like something solid, and across the flattened fields, and over the ridge into Godhanger Wood to set its myriad trees thrashing and dancing to the music that sang of autumn's end and the coming of winter.

Everywhere within the creaking, groaning, straining wood, the air was thick with falling leaves of all sizes and patterns – the lance-blades of ash and the heart shapes of sycamore, the smooth oval leaves of the beech and the great spinning five-lobed fronds of the horse chestnut, with a dozen other kinds besides, all wrenched from their last weak hold on life by the westerly, and sent swirling and swaying and circling down to the floor of the wood.

All that night the gale came flying un-checked across thousands of miles of sea, and at first light on the following morning, great white clouds of seabirds rode upon its power, high above the straining trees of Godhanger. Hundreds, thou-sands of gulls, whirled silently inland in search of food and shelter, rising, falling, banking, curvet-ting, as they danced on the wind's wildness.

By next nightfall much of the wood was stripped naked as, squadron after squadron, the fleet of gulls returned seawards, calling to one another 'Ha-Ha-Ha!' in their harsh voices. A gang of rooks whirled over on their way home to roost after fieldwork, and saw below a patchwork of quite new colours, for the browns and greys of the bare flayed trees were broken only by the odd stand of conifers, the darkness of holly and yew, and the great evergreen cedars and cypresses in the grove. As the light died, so did the wind, and the wood was becoming still once more when Gilbert the wild cat came down from his nest in the ruined oak.

Reaching the ground, he turned his back upon the trunk, and, raising his tail, marked his precious territory with a sudden squirting spray. Then, treading delicately amongst the newfallen leaves, he made off through the trees, the tip of his barred tail curling from one side to the other, as though it had a life of its own.

Two pairs of eyes watched that tail-tip until it disappeared from sight. Then two young dog-foxes stepped out from a patch of ferns in whose cover they had been crouching.

Flem and Fitz had not yet reached maturity but no longer thought of themselves as cubs. The grey-brown woolly coats that they had worn since their birth in the early spring had changed to yellow-brown fur, and only a certain gawky ranginess showed them to be not yet full-grown. But already, in the eight months of their lives, they had learned much of death.

They had never known their father (he had met with a hunting accident, their mother told them), and not long after they and their two litter-sisters had been weaned, the vixen herself went out to hunt one evening and never returned to the earth. Darcy the carrion crow could have told them of her last resting-place, the gibbet, where she hung, head down and wasp-waisted from the squeezing of the snare that had held her. But all they knew was that no more food was brought to them, so that they must needs fend for themselves.

For a while the four little cubs managed, catching an occasional mouse or frog but existing mainly on beetles and worms, until one early morning when, returning home, they did not notice a figure as motionless and as greeny-brown as the tree trunk behind which it stood. Two shots rang out, two fox cubs lay dead, and Flem and Fitz ran and ran through Godhanger till their trembling legs would carry them no further.

Somehow they survived. One day when they were at their lowest ebb, tired, bewildered and empty-bellied, they had a stroke of luck. A great and strange bird flew over them, and by some odd chance let fall before their very noses the body of a hare. A big jack-hare it had been, a good five kilos in weight, and it lasted Flem and Fitz for quite a time. More than that, this godsend seemed to mark a turning point in their struggle, and from that time on they began to grow fast, in cunning as in stature, hunting always in company, each his brother's keeper.

Now, as they emerged from the ferns, they were the very picture of alertness. Heads raised and turning all about, ears fanned, muzzles testing the breeze, Flem and Fitz walked to the base of the ruined oak. By nose, they inspected the cat's marking.

'Pissycat!' said Flem, wrinkling his lip.

'Let us improve upon it,' said Fitz, grinning, and in solemn turn they cocked their legs against Gilbert's precious tree. Simultaneously, as so often happened, an idea occurred to them.

'Let's have a bit of fun . . .' said Flem.

'. . . and follow him,' said Fitz.

The foxes had no liking for the wild cat – a competitor and an evil-tempered one at that – and the thought of a little tom-teasing appealed to their sense of mischief.

'He went upwind,' said Fitz.

'The moon will be rising soon,' said Flem.

'And you never know,' said Fitz. 'He might just catch something . . .'

'. . . of which we could relieve him,' said Flem.

'Let him do the work, brother.'

'And we, brother, will reap the reward.'

And off they set on Gilbert's trail in their customary formation, one scouting ahead, nose to ground, the other as rear guard, watchful head raised as he trotted ten metres behind his twin.

In fact, Gilbert was going to the midden.

At the back of the gamekeeper's cottage was a narrow strip of garden where he grew a few vegetables, and at the top end of the strip stood a rough square of broken walling that had once been the outer run of a long-collapsed pigsty.

Here the gamekeeper threw all manner of rubbish – empty bottles and tins, bones from his stockpot and other kitchen waste, dead-in-shell chicks and addled eggs in the pheasant-rearing season, and the bodies of a whole variety of creatures that had died at his hands by one means or another, and either did not merit or could not be afforded a place on the gibbet. As for the tenants of the gallows themselves, once they had hung there long enough to serve as a warning to others, the rotten bundles of fur or feather were also pitched upon the midden, in the very heart of which, in a complex of tunnels, lived a small colony of rats.

Despite, or perhaps because of the nearness

of the cottage – for unlike other creatures in Godhanger, there was in the cat-gone-wild an instinct that drew him back to man's haunts – Gilbert came often here to hunt the scavengers.

In particular, he aspired to put an end to Rawden the master-rat, a big fat old yellow-toothed buck who had thus far always escaped him. In Gilbert's view, there was about Rawden a barefaced cheek that infuriated him. On several occasions the old rat had showed those yellow teeth and actually chattered – in anger, if you please, not fear – at him, before diving fatly to safety. If there was one woodlander that Gilbert loathed fraction-ally more than the rest, it was Rawden.

So obsessed was he by this thought on this particular night that he trotted directly towards the end of the cottage garden without a single stop to investigate various rustlings and other small night-noises beside his path, so that the foxes did not catch up with him. They followed his line faultlessly, but by the time Fitz, who was leading, first spotted him in the light of the risen moon, Gilbert was already in position, sitting bolt upright and stock-still on top of the wall of the broken pigsty, staring fixedly down.

Flem drew level with his brother and saw also, without the need to be told. They paused for a moment and tested the wind that brought them a heady mixture of cat and of rat and of many dead and rotting things. Then, again without a word spoken, they split up and moved nearer to the midden, slowly, silently, watching from either flank the motionless Gilbert. Still downwind of him, they stopped and waited.

Minutes passed and none of the three animals stirred. Then suddenly Gilbert tensed, and all in one flowing movement leapt down into the midden and back up again on to the wall. Dangling from his jaws was something plump that kicked and twirled madly, its long bare tail whirling round and round. Held by the throat, Rawden could neither bite nor cry out, and Gilbert was about to put an end to him when a sharp muzzle rose from the nettles beside the wall.

'That's a big fat one,' said Fitz pleasantly, and from the other side of the pigsty Flem added, 'Give it here, pissycat, we'll have that.'

Instinctively Gilbert opened his jaws in a snarling hiss of rage. He held on to Rawden with both forepaws, but the old rat immediately began a terrible squealing, that in turn set the dog barking in its kennel behind the cottage. Simultaneously Flem, who had jumped over into the midden, and Fitz from without, began to tease the furious wild cat, snapping at him from either side as he stood upon his prey, in an attempt to make him release it.

Suddenly, through the kerfuffle, the sharp ears of the two foxes caught a sound, a stealthy but distinctive sound, and immediately they melted away into the trees. It was the sound of a window-sash being raised.

Gilbert did not hear it. He was beside himself with anger. Hunched upon the wall in the bright moonlight, Rawden still struggling in his grasp, the cat continued to scream and yowl at his tormentors. His back was turned to the cottage and he never saw the glint of the gun barrels, nor, it must be presumed, heard the crash of the shot.

As the charge hit him, once again that barred tail lifted vertically and ramrod-straight, but now the fluid that marked this last territory was blood, as he pitched forward into the midden and lay still. From under his broken body, the old rat Rawden emerged stiffly and staggered away to disappear down a runway into the warm bowels of the heap of rotting rubbish.

Silence settled once again over Godhanger, except for the calls of the owls that told, as ever, of death.

## CHAPTER FOUR

The owls were usually the first of the followers to arrive in the cedar of Lebanon for the dawn meeting. Glyde the tawny owl, in particular, cared little for the broad light of day when, if he went late to roost, a crowd of small birds was wont to mob him, fluttering in his very face and calling him rude names.

The little owl Eustace was in fact often about in the daytime, but even so preferred to come early to the cedar, looking forward by then to a snooze after his night's hunting.

The third to come was, as a rule, Darcy the carrion crow, having risen at the first peep of light to inspect the gibbet.

The following morning was grey and cold. The wind had risen a little, blowing now from the north, and the branch of the cedar on which the two owls already sat lifted and fell with a regular gentle movement like the swell of the sea.

Glyde, to whom dignity meant much, bore this motion with a somewhat pained look, but Eustace was enjoying it and gave a little extra hop of pleasure at the top of each upswing.

'Where's everybody?' he said to Glyde. 'Are we the first? Where's the Master?'

Glyde chose not to answer, merely adopting a rather sour expression. Privately he thought Eustace an impudent creature, and besides, the sway of the branch was not helping him to digest the contents of a full crop.

At that moment Darcy came flying in and landed between them. His expression was more than usually funereal.

'Important news,' he croaked. 'Guess what.'

'You're going to have a baby,' said Eustace, happily bouncing.

'If I may say so,' said Glyde, 'that was a very foolish remark, Eustace. First, it is the wrong season of the year, and second, Darcy is a cock bird.'

'Ah, silly me!' said Eustace. 'Of course you're right, Glyde. As always. Let's try again.'

'It was something that I've just seen,' said Darcy. 'Something amazing.'

'I know!' said Eustace cheerfully. 'You saw the Master eating an earthworm when he thought no one was looking.'

'Eustace!' cried Glyde in a voice full of horror at such effrontery. 'Whatever would our Master think if he could hear you?'

'He'd probably think it was funny,' said Eustace. 'He has a sense of humour, you know.' He dropped his voice. 'Unlike some people,' he said out of the side of his mouth.

'I do not think,' said Darcy, 'that the Master would stoop to such a thing.'

Bored, Eustace yawned. 'Oh, all right, I give up,' he said. 'What did you see?'

The crow settled himself importantly. He looked at each owl in turn to assure himself of their full attention and then opened his beak to reply.

At that instant they all heard a loud shrieking carried on the wind. It was the voice of the hen jay, the crier of all news, as she made the rounds of Godhanger Wood.

'Skraaak!' she cried. 'Cat's dead! Cat's dead! Skraaak!'

'Hey, wait a minute, Darcy,' said Eustace as the screams of the gaudy widow died away in the distance. 'I think I've got it! You saw that old moggy and he's copped it. Where?'

'On the midden,' said Darcy sourly.

'Aaaaah!' said Eustace sardonically, as the flap

and flutter of many wings was heard, and, one after another, there flew into the branches of the cedar of Lebanon the rest of the followers of the Skymaster. The magpie came first, perching as always high and watchful, followed by the buzzards and a smaller member of their tribe, a sparrowhawk. Then came two more of the crow family, Jeb the grey-pated jackdaw and his mate, and after them, two falcons — a hobby and a kestrel. Soon the whole company of followers, eleven in all, were settled in the cedar in all their variety of colour, shape and size.

For a moment there was silence in the tree. Glyde was considering giving the morning greeting himself in the absence of the Master, when they all heard a deep voice high above.

'Krok! Krok!' said the voice, and then in among them dropped the mightiest of the crows. Now there were twelve.

'Loftus!' said Glyde in a tone of amazement. 'What are you doing here?'

'Do you object?' said Loftus.

'Oh, no,' said Glyde hastily.

'We are glad to see you,' said Darcy, and most of the others made small noises that might have signified agreement. Only the buzzards appeared uncomfortable.

Loftus looked about him in the branches.

'Where is he?' he said.

'No doubt he is about his business,' said Glyde unctuously. Now, he thought, I'll give the greeting now. It will impress this newcomer.

'My friends,' he said, but before he could go further, Eustace bounced closer to the raven and said in a confidential voice, 'The cat's dead.'

Loftus looked blank.

'Didn't you hear the jaybird?' said Jeb the jackdaw.

'Dead on the midden, she was saying,' said the hobby.

'Shot to bits, she was saying,' said the kestrel.

'Didn't you know?' asked the sparrowhawk.

'I know nothing of it,' said Loftus curtly to the woodland birds. 'I came in from the heights where no jay flies. What cat is this? Cats and dogs are man's creatures.'

'This one is of the wood,' Darcy said. 'He is one of us.'

'Was,' said Eustace shortly.

'Is that why you are all gathered?' asked Loftus, turning to the buzzards.

'Whee-oo, we are, we are,' they chorused mournfully.

'To hear what he has to say about it? The

death of an old cat? Does he then concern himself with such a thing?'

'With any and every death,' said Glyde. 'A sparrow does not fall to the ground without his knowing.'

'And all of you come here, each day, to hear him?'

'Not all of us,' said Glyde a trifle primly.

'But you yourself do?' said Loftus. 'Every day?'

The tawny owl shifted on his perch. 'Actually I didn't come yesterday,' he said. 'The gale . . . it was blowing so strongly . . .'

'Did any of you?' asked the raven, but no one answered. They do not know then, thought Loftus, of the Skymaster's injury. Could it be that he has not come today because of it? Has it worsened so that he cannot fly? Could it be that he is . . . dead?

At this last thought he gave an involuntary shudder, but even as he did so, Myles' loud chattering call came from the tree top.

'He is coming!' called down the magpie. 'Welcome, Master!'

Loftus watched intently as the Skymaster glided into the dark depths of the cedar of Lebanon. The wing looked strong and mended. He anticipated some reference to the matter, expected perhaps to be publicly thanked for his part in the affair, and was a little nettled when the Skymaster paid not the slightest attention to him on this, his first attendance, but launched straight into the morning greeting. All then moved nearer to their Master, leaving the raven sitting alone, and a babble of talk began. Loftus perforce kept his beak shut and listened to the shrill excited voices.

'The cat is killed, Master!'

'Gilbert is dead!'

'The old moggy's copped it!'

'The jaybird said so!'

'On the midden, she said!'

'Shot to bits, she said!'

'I saw it first, Master, I saw it first!'

'Good riddance, I say!'

'He'll kill no more nestlings!'

'Murdering monster!'

'Bad-tempered brute!'

'Miserable old creature!'

Throughout this hubbub the Skymaster sat silent, his head bowed, his eyes closed, as his followers ranted on. Is this then the meekness that the buzzards spoke of, thought Loftus? Has he no control over this chattering mob? Where is this power of which they speak?

And then suddenly the great bird drew himself up to his full height, eyes ablaze with anger.

'Be silent!' cried the Skymaster in an awful voice, and they were silent.

'And listen!' And they listened.

'You have learned nothing,' he said (and his words were the more terrible because now they were spoken softly), 'since first I came among you. You make a mockery of death, of the death of a fellow-creature, of the death that waits for each and every one of you. I hope that when it comes, it is not as harsh as Gilbert's. Friendless he lived and friendless he died.'

He turned his head and looked at each, slowly, searchingly, and none, of course, looked back. 'I wish you better fortune,' he said. None answered.

'Loftus,' said the Skymaster.

'Yes, Master?'

'Stay with me. The rest of you, go!' And away they lifted in silent haste: the owls, the crows, the hawks, the falcons, till only the ancient and the ageless sat together in the cedar of Lebanon.

'So you have come at last,' said the Skymaster, and now he sounded angry no longer, but only tired.

'If I am not too old to learn from you,' said

the raven. 'But to learn, I must first understand. What have the others done thus to merit your anger?'

'They revel in the death of a fellow animal.'

'A bad-tempered old tom-cat?'

'He was one of us,' said the Skymaster shortly, and he stretched out one great wing and then refolded it.

The action caused Loftus' mind to jump to a practical matter. 'How is your injury?'

'Healing, Loftus. Healing well, thanks to your surgery. And I rested it throughout the gale.'

So you didn't come here yesterday either, thought Loftus.

'No,' said the Skymaster, just as though the raven had spoken, 'I did not come here yesterday. Glyde and the others need not have worried.'

He knows everything, Loftus thought. I do not understand. 'Was it for one of them,' he said, 'that you risked your life?'

'No. For another.'

'And they do not know of it?'

'No. Only you know.'

'And you wish it kept secret between the two of us?'

'That is a matter for you to decide, my friend,' said the Skymaster. 'Perhaps you wish your good deed to be known?'

Loftus saw that he could say nothing of the matter without seeming to praise himself for his part in it. 'No, no, of course not,' he said. 'It was a little thing that I did.' Then he felt a sudden glow of pride that he alone knew, that he sat alone now in the heart of the cedar of Lebanon with the great strange bird of Godhanger. Suddenly there was so much that the old raven wanted to know about him: where he was born, and of whom, and why he had come to this one place, to this ancient wood in a combe close by the western sea.

'I will tell you,' said the Skymaster, again as though the thoughts had been words. 'Come, sit beside me.'

Ah, thought Loftus, side by side I need not lower my gaze before his. But who will guard our backs?

'You will be more comfortable thus,' said the Skymaster. 'And Myles or Darcy will sound the alarm if needs be.'

'Or the jaybird,' said Loftus.

'Or the jaybird indeed. Settle yourself and listen.'


'The country of my birth', said the Skymaster, 'lies many hundreds of miles to the north, a wild lonely country of mountain and glen and forest, of cold clear rivers and deep still lakes. It is the land of the red deer that roam the high tops, and of the red grouse that whirr above the heather-coated moors. It is a land that is often harsh and windswept, where the snow lies year-round on the highest peaks. Yet its beauty is unsur-passed, and unforgettable to those fortunate enough to call it home. There, on a rocky ledge on the sheer side of the highest of the moun-tains of those high lands, was a nest built of pine-branches and twigs, lined with heather-tufts and moss and grass, and in its cup was a single egg.

'From this egg I broke, at the dawn of a bright, cold morning of spring. Naked I was, like any new-hatched nestling, and stiff and tottery from the cramp of my prison, but I had the gift of sight from my first-drawn breath. I see it now as clearly as then.

'It is the ruins of the egg that I first recall, shattered marbled fragments blotched with reddish-brown and violet, fragments still warm, as I was, from the brooding of the great bird that stood above me, and bent, and gently touched me with her huge hooked bill. I see her move away and stand upon the rim of the nest, and throw back her head, and I hear the loud yelping scream that she gave and another that answered it from on high.

'Majestic she was; her strong legs feathered to the toes, her plumage tawny, with the glow on the nape of her proud neck, of that golden colour that gives her kind its name.

'This was my mother, who gave me birth and sheltered and fed me, and soon down beside her dropped her mate, a little smaller as is the way with that breed, but as noble in look, with his massive head and heavy brow and piercing eyes. And on that rocky eyrie, highest birthplace of birds, they looked down together at this, their first hatchling.

'And presently, when the sun was newly risen, there came to the eyrie three strangers to stand beside them and look upon the baby that sprawled among the eggshell. Them, too, I can clearly see.

'One was a little bird of the woods. Brick-red in colour, with dark wings, its tail was short and forked, and its beak was like no other, the upper mandible crossed over the lower.

'One was a black-and-white sea-bird. Stumpy and big-headed, its bill again was of the oddest kind, a large flattened triangle brilliantly striped in red, blue and yellow.

'The third was a long-legged bird of the moorlands. Once more, its bill was of the strangest shape, very slender and down-curving and near half the length of its buff-streaked body.

'And each of these three birds carried an offering in its singular beak. The crossbill brought a pine-cone, the puffin a seashell, and the curlew a sprig of purple bell-heather.

'These tokens they dropped into my nest, and for a while looked upon me, and then turned and flew back into the northern sky. Of how they found me I knew nothing. But later, when I was fledged, my mother told me that on the night before my hatching the sky had been ablaze with strange lights, long tremulous streamers of many colours that had led the three birds to me, from dark forest, windswept cliff and desolate moor.

'In the weeks that followed my birth day I grew strong in the care of the two great birds. But they knew I was no ordinary fledgling.

'Then, after three moons had waxed and waned, the unforgettable day dawned, the day of first flight.

'You will remember, Loftus, how it was with you – all those hours of wing-beating, strongly and yet more strongly, lifting a little from the nest yet still not daring to leave it, till at last the moment comes. Somewhere high above me the two great birds soared, somewhere far below me there walked or crawled or hopped all those beasts that never know the joy of flight, when I launched myself from the shoulder of the world.

'This, not the clumsy hatching, is the true birth of a bird, as you well know. This is the miracle that divides us from all other creatures, when first we lie upon the cradling air and feel the updraught hold and lift us, in the element that is ours alone.

'All of us feel this ecstasy, but I, I felt more, for with the ecstasy came power, limitless power, so that with hardly a wing-beat I rose ever upward, circling effortlessly higher and higher into the blue sky, until I reached heights that no bird had ever known, so that the mountains below were no more than the ant-heaps in a meadow and I could glimpse the shimmer of the sea at the land's edges.

'And as I hung and floated there, I saw below a great shadow that came drifting across the face of the earth beneath, like the passing of a huge cloud. Over the sunlit land this shadow moved, fashioned in the shape of a mighty bird with wings outstretched. But when I looked above me, the sky was still and empty and cloudless, and when I bent my head once more, the shadow was gone.

'I dropped earthwards once more, and came again to the eyrie, and found the two great birds there. And I cried farewell to them, and to that wild lonely country, and straightway set out to the south, coming at last to the place called Godhanger.

'Since then, Loftus, I have lived here among you.'

In the silence that followed, they heard in the distance the chattering warning of the magpie Myles.

'Go now,' said the Skymaster, 'back to your sea-cliffs, for the gamekeeper is abroad. Go, Loftus.'

'Master,' said Loftus, '*you* will never go?' and to his dying day, he remembered the words of the reply.

'I will never leave you,' said the Skymaster.

## CHAPTER FIVE

Days later, Loftus and his mate were feasting upon the carcase of a sheep. Usually their scavenging was confined to less generous offerings, rabbits at best, though in the lambing season they could rely upon the afterbirths of newly-dropped lambs and the bodies of the stillborn.

But now they had found the corpse of a ewe that had been cast, had rolled upon her back, that is, in a slight hollow on the grass of a clifftop field, and had been unable to right herself. After a while the weight of her innards had compressed her lungs and she had died.

Once they had pecked out the eyeballs, the ravens used their great bills to break into the body and drag out the guts.

Sated at last, the hen bird flapped heavily away, and Loftus was about to follow when he saw a distant figure rise out of Godhanger and fly westward towards him with slow, majestic wing-beats.

Minutes later the Skymaster landed beside him on the sheep-nibbled turf. 'Rich pickings, Loftus,' he said.

'I must live on such fare,' said Loftus. 'Not for me fresh-killed prey such as sparrowhawks or falcons take. I would offer you some, but . . .'

'But what? I too am a scavenger, did you not know? Like you, I must eat whatever I can find in order to survive. I should be grateful for a share in your bounty.'

'Oh, please, Master!' said Loftus. 'Please help yourself.'

For a while they fed side by side in silence, the great black bird and the greater tawny one, the dagger bill and the hooked beak tearing at the cold flesh of the dead ewe, until each had eaten his fill.

Then, 'Shall we fly together, Loftus?' said the Skymaster, and they took off and floated away, out of the field, over the hedges, over the clifftop, over the raven's ledge where now his mate sat, digesting her meal.

'Prruk!' called Loftus in his deep voice, and in answer she gave a high metallic 'Tok!'

'You are fortunate,' said the Skymaster as they sailed out over the sea. 'I have no mate.'

Searching for some reply to this remark, Loftus, without thinking, turned his head towards his companion. To his great surprise he found that, whereas on earth he could not look upon the other, here, in their own element, the air, he could. And now, for the first time, he focused fully upon the huge dark shape.

Wedge-tailed, broad wings spread, the Skymaster sailed effortlessly beside the raven, and Loftus, looking upon him unafraid, could see at close quarters the great hooked beak with its yellow cere, and the terrible talons on the yellow feet, and, on the back of the head, the nape of feathers as golden as the morning sun.

The sea that day was as calm as it can ever be in those parts. The waves that broke upon the pebble-strewn shore were gentle, and the two birds flew on out over a blue-black surface whose only movement was the slow, barely perceptible rise and fall of a long swell, as though the ocean were quietly breathing.

Below them they could see a number of round, dark, doglike heads sticking up out of the water. The grey seals knew Loftus well enough, but they stared with their prominent eyes in a kind of amazement at sight of the raven's great companion.

'Hoo!' cried several in their melancholy voices.

'The sea is in a kindly mood today, is it not?' said the Skymaster as they flew further out.

'For a change,' said Loftus. 'It is not often so at this season of the year.'

It was indeed a peerless winter's day, with little wind, a cloudless sky and bright sunshine. Certainly it was cold, but the two felt it not through the shield of their tight feathering.

'In your long life, Loftus,' the Skymaster said, 'you must have seen the sea in all its moods.'

'Indeed,' replied the raven. 'It can wear a pleasant face, as now, but it can be very cruel.'

'Like life,' said the other. 'You never know what the next day may bring – content or worry, triumph or disappointment, safety and security or hardship and danger. Death even.'

'I never thought about death when I was young,' said Loftus. 'Now that I am old, very old, I wonder – is there something beyond?'

'So I believe,' said the Skymaster. 'So, one day, may you.'

For a while the raven kept silence. Then he said, 'Let us not talk of death, Master, on such a day as this.'

'You are right, Loftus,' said the Skymaster.

'Let us enjoy life while we can. Old you may be, but I doubt that you have lost your skills in the air. I am only a stately soarer, but you, I know, have the art of aerobatics at your wingtips. Show me.'

And Loftus was taken with a sudden joy in the beauty of the day, in the freedom of the air, in the friendship of the great strange bird of Godhanger Wood whose words had somehow filled him with hope. He felt strong and confident, as in his youth, and while the watching Skymaster circled slowly, wide wings outspread, high above the glassy sea, the old bird treated him to a dazzling display of a raven's aerial agility.

First he gained height, to float above the other, circling in time with him. Then, suddenly, he shot down past him with half-closed wings, turning and twisting with great rapidity. Next, he began to roll in horizontal flight, turning belly upwards, sometimes with wings clamped, sometimes not tightly shut, and repeatedly recovering into a normal flight position. Time and again he rolled thus, in a reverse corkscrew motion, varying this manoeuvre with the occasional somersault or figure of eight, until at last he tired and broke off.

'Bravo!' cried the Skymaster, coming to join

him. 'You have gladdened my heart, Loftus!' And he threw back his head and gave his strange yelping cry.

Together they beat slowly back towards the now distant land, over the quietly heaving sea, over the staring seals, over the raven's cliff-ledge where his mate cried to him as before and he answered.

'Go to her now, Loftus,' said the Skymaster, and he flew on towards Godhanger.

Loftus circled a moment, watching him, and even as he watched, the light easterly breeze carried to his ears familiar sounds from the distant woods. Gunshots.

Despite his invariable expression which was fierce and frowning, Eustace was a jolly person. Also, he was (he considered) level-headed, and well-qualified to pass judgement on other creatures in Godhanger Wood. Like all little owls, he was often about the place in broad daylight which gave him (he suspected) a more balanced view of things than had those who thought of themselves as strictly nocturnal or the reverse, and made him (he felt confident) a connoisseur of character. He sat dozing now in the entrance to his home, a hole in an ash tree, when the magpie's alarm-call rang out higher up the wood and brought him back to wakefulness.

Noisy fellow, Myles, he thought, noisy and nefarious and never still, and he began to amuse himself by composing a mental report on the others who had gathered that morning in the cedar of Lebanon. First, there's old Glyde, of course – well, I don't want to be hard on a fellow owl but he is the wood's biggest bore, thought Eustace. Pompous, that's the word for Glyde, and what's more, I suspect he's not half as clever as he thinks he is.

Now Darcy, he's no fool – none of the crow family are, of course, whether it's Myles or that jackdaw Jeb and his mate – but Darcy's not a lot of fun: gloomy old sobersides, nothing he likes more than telling you how many corpses there are on the gibbet.

And talking about gloomy – you couldn't find a more dismal pair than those buzzards, it's moan, moan, moan all day long.

I'm not too keen on the three smaller ones either – there's the sparrowhawk dashing about the place in that show-off way his lot have, the hobby's the same only faster, and the kestrel's just the opposite, hovering, hovering, always hovering, you'd think it'd drive him mad.

Who've I left out? Oh yes, of course, the raven. Now I wonder why he was kept behind this morning? I bet old Glyde didn't like that; thinks he's the Master's right-wing bird, old Glyde does, but that raven's as clever as ten tawny owls and powerful with it, shouldn't like a tap on the head from him, great ugly black monster.

In fact, thought Eustace happily, I don't really give a pellet for any of them, and as if to underline his opinion, he disgorged one, and watched it fall at the foot of the ash. Except, of course, for the Skymaster, he remembered. Now what is it that I feel for him?

I respect him, I admire him, I trust him, I think of him as my friend. But above all, I suppose, I am in awe of him. It is not fear, there is none of that for I know he wouldn't harm a feather of my head. It is a kind of wonder. In his presence, I am a very little owl.

Myles' warning sounded again, much closer, followed by the crash of two gunshots, and Eustace's musings changed abruptly from the metaphysical to the matter-of-fact.

Whereas sitting out here in full view may lead to my being a very *dead* little owl, he thought, and he shuffled backwards into the concealing darkness of his den.

His sense of hearing was very acute, and before long he caught the sound of footsteps (not even the gamekeeper could move silently through dry crackly leaves), and then, very near, the snuffling of a dog. The spaniel nosed among the litter of owl-pellets that lay beneath the ash-tree hole, but found nothing attractive in these last arid remnants of beetle, mouse or shrew, and soon pattered away.

After a while, a dove in a nearby tree began its three-note lullaby – 'Coo-*coo*-coo, coo-*coo*-coo' – which Eustace took as a sure sign of danger past, and he settled his round head comfortably upon his shoulders, shut his yellow eyes, and went to sleep.

All through the length and breadth of Godhanger, the animals reacted to the movements of the gamekeeper. Most of those on his route, like Eustace and his neighbour the dove, kept quiet and still. Some, like Baldwin the badger and the foxes, Flem and Fitz, already slept, safe below ground: Baldwin heavily, upon his side, snoring, the foxes more lightly, their long muzzles tucked into their flanks, their thick white-tipped brushes curled cosily around, but their senses alert, even in sleep, for the slightest sound, the faintest smell.

Some, like the small singing birds, kept their distance but otherwise paid little heed. But for many, caught off guard, safety lay solely in silence and immobility. The squirrel flattened against the reverse side of a tree trunk, the roe deer standing like a statue in the thicket, the rabbit frozen behind the tussock: all were only safe if still. For each, to lose its nerve might be to lose its life. The rule was a simple one. To live, stay still as death.

But as always, danger, this danger, could not be in two places at once, and usually the wood-landers knew, roughly by the cry of jay or crow or magpie, or exactly by the clap of gunshot, whereabouts the gamekeeper was in the course of his patrol.

Thus, that morning, there were a number of creatures busy about the clearing in which the cottage stood, confident that they had a little time to play with before the return of its occupant.

From their lookout point on top of its single chimney stack, the two jackdaws flew down into the sour-floored, rust-wired chicken run to steal food from the dozen fat old fowls that the gamekeeper kept to lay for him when they could be bothered but principally to go broody (something they were only too willing to do) and hatch out, in the pheasant-rearing season, other more valuable eggs.

'Jack! Jack!' cried the 'daws, and crammed their crops with the golden berries of wheat, while the hens fussed and fumed, fluffing out feathers and making clumsy runs at them which they nimbly dodged.

Farther up the strip of garden was a plot where the gamekeeper grew some vegetables, but they were few, as he could seldom be bothered. It was weedy and unkempt, but it did contain his particular favourites, Brussels sprouts.

There were a couple of short rows of them, now, with the first frosts not far off, at their best and ready for picking. Indeed, they *were* being picked, by an animal no taller than the plants themselves. His coat that had been foxy-red in summer, now longer and greyer against the onset of winter, the roe deer buck greedily wrenched off the tight round sprout-buttons with a twist of his little head that was elegantly antlered, three points a side, and swallowed them hastily. Later, in safety and at his ease, he would lie and chew the cud, but now speed was of the essence.

Soon his hornless mate came lightly bouncing down the garden to join the feast, followed by her two white-spotted fawns of that year. When the roe family had done with the gamekeeper's precious sprouts, there was precious little of them left.

'Daw and deer were not the only robbers. At the top of the garden strip there stood a walnut tree, whose roots had, over the years, contributed to the downfall of the pigsty wall, against which it grew. Here a pair of squirrels were hard at work, for the walnuts were ripe for harvesting, and the two of them shuttled continuously backward and forward along the top of the broken wall. In turn, each leapt into the tree, found a nut and bit it off with sharp incisors, and, mouthing the prize, ran back in its curious flat spread-legged way, long bushy tail rippling behind, and jumped down and away into the surrounding cover. Wisely, the squirrels planned to hoard the nuts against the thin times of winter, but, foolishly, they always chose so many hiding-places that they forgot where most were stored.

Below them as they worked, several brown shapes moved about the surface of the midden, scaly tails dragging behind them, sharp, whiskered muzzles investigating anything remotely edible. These were all doe-rats, for the old buck Rawden would tolerate no competition, and always, before his sons could reach maturity, he drove them fiercely away, out into the wide wood to seek their fortunes, or, to put it differently, to take their chances with the stoats and the weasels and the tawny owls. Even in hard times he himself seldom went hungry: throughout the year there was usually an emergency supply of food close at hand, somewhere in the depths of the midden, for Rawden was a cannibal. Only the previous day, because he was still too bruised from Gilbert's mauling to forage, he had killed and eaten a nest of his own children, a dozen of them, fat, pink, blind and hairless, to build up his strength. Now, he felt the benefit and the need for a different kind of tonic, and he made his way out through a drainhole at the bottom of the wall, and walked, a little stiffly still, down the garden towards the chicken run, taking no notice of the raiding roe deer but alert as always for danger from the sky.

Once at the regular runway that led underneath the henhouse, Rawden moved with great care. Sometimes there would be a trap, a wooden break-back thing like a mousetrap, but much bigger, with a heavy spring-arm, baited perhaps with a piece of bacon rind. Not a few of his family, the young and the foolish, had died in its jaws.

But Rawden was neither young nor foolish,

and only when he was completely satisfied that the runway was clear did he slip under the henhouse and up into its interior by way of a hole gnawed beside the row of apple-crates that served as nest boxes. Several were occupied by broody birds who fluffed themselves out and grizzled angrily at the old rat. But towards the end of the row he found an egg.

A lesser rat might have broken and eaten it on the spot, but Rawden had no wish to stay a moment longer than need be, and with the ease of long practice he manoeuvred the egg out of the nest box, onto the floor, through the hole, and down into the runway.

But it was once he was clear of the henhouse and faced with the straight run up the garden to the midden that the rat really showed his skill. Holding the egg tucked between chin and forepaws, Rawden trundled it along as easily as though it were a perfect sphere instead of its actual awkward shape, until he came to the drainhole, and so to the mouth of his burrow in the heap. Only then did he break it, slobbering at it greedily till his whiskers were sticky with yolk. One of his does had the temerity to approach him in hopes of a share of such a breakfast, but a furious squeal from Rawden sent her scuttling, and reached the ears of Darcy, sitting as usual on the gibbet.

As it happened, the gibbet was disappointingly bare. There were no fresh corpses, and those that still hung there were desiccated. Rawden's squealing made Darcy think of the attractions of fresh rat-meat. He looked up at his mate, on guard as usual, but she was silent, so he flew down on to the pigsty wall, causing the squirrels to disappear at speed. He did not expect to surprise an adult rat, but in the past he had had some luck with part-grown youngsters, newly emerged from their nest into the light of day. At first, he knew, they moved about quite slowly and uncertainly, and it was an easy matter to knock one or two on the head before they could get below again.

In fact, only Rawden was to be seen, finishing his egg. At sight of the crow, he stood up on his hind legs and yakkered in fury, but when Darcy hopped down, the old buck forgot his age and stiffness, and whisked into his hole.

Darcy ate the eggshell, and was beginning to walk about the surface of the midden when he heard his name called.

'Daaaaaar-cy!' croaked his mate, and simultaneously there came two other alarm calls, 'Jack, jack, jack, jack!' from Jeb on the chimney stack, and a sharp bark from the roe buck.

The kestrel, hovering thirty metres above, saw the clearing suddenly empty. He turned and flew away to a safer remove as the gamekeeper came out of the wood, his dog at heel. Immediately she ran past him and down the garden, quartering the ground among the Brussels sprouts and wagging her plumed tail in high excitement.

The kestrel saw the man follow, saw him bend, first to inspect the slot-marks in the earth about the plants, and then the plants themselves. He saw him tear off his shapeless hat and hurl it on the ground and pick it up again to ease his anger by using it to belabour the rump of the eagerly questing spaniel.

Shocked, the dog ran yelping, tail beneath her, into her kennel.

Furious, the man crammed his hat back on his head and stalked away into his cottage.

Interested no longer, the kestrel slid away down the wind.

So there was no one left to see when, presently, the gamekeeper came out of his door once more. He was carrying, not his trusty shot-gun, but a rifle. He called his dog who came running to him, fawning lest her recent strange ill-treatment be repeated, but then delighted to receive instead a pat and a pulling of her long silky ears. A length of cord was attached to her collar, and she was encouraged back to the Brussels sprouts and urged about the business which only moments before had earned her a smacking.

Now more than usually anxious to please, and whining in her eagerness, she quickly found the line of the roe deer, and away went the pair into the depths of Godhanger.

Only the comfortable clucking of the hens now broke the silence of the clearing, and soon the squirrels came running back along the pigsty wall.

The temper of the gamekeeper was in no way improved by the sudden arrival of the jay, who chanced upon the hunters before they had gone far into the wood, and flew, as usual, two gunshots in front of them, yelling, 'Skraaak! It's the murderer! Watch out, everyone!' She was not to know that each time she pitched and looked back towards them, she was well within the range of the rifle; but though the angry gamekeeper was sorely tempted, he did not shoot, hoping that she would tire and go away before the deer were alerted. But she did not and they were, for she flapped noisily straight towards the spot where they had chosen to lie and cud.

Instantly there took place what was patently a well-rehearsed drill. Without panic but in haste the family bounded off between the trees, the buck leading, followed by his doe and the two five-month-old fawns. The adults made several high leaps, looking back.

After a couple of hundred metres they stopped at a point where the path they were following began to be bordered by an area of tall thick bracken; then, at some unseen signal, the fawns ran on a little way in front of their parents and suddenly, as one, leaped sideways off the path to lie still in the dense cover. There, trained to do so since birth, they would remain until such time as their mother should return to tell them all was clear; they would couch in the bracken, moving no muscle, giving out hardly any scent, their coats blending into the russet and gold of the fronds. The only way for an enemy to find them was to step on them. As soon as the fawns were out of sight the roe buck and his doe turned sharply at right angles, away from the bracken, off the path, and ran downwind together. But before very long they separated, the doe forking to her left towards the distant grove, the buck to his right, making for the nose part of Godhanger's horsehead shape, where the stream that threaded the combe skirted the wood closely.

Now the jay was silent. Her mission was to warn the hunted, not to help the hunters, and when the dog reached the bracken patch the only sound to be heard was the distant drumming of a great spotted woodpecker on a dead bough.

The spaniel overran the point where the four deer had halted till she was level with the fawns' hiding-place. Here she checked, cast about the path for a moment, ran back on the heel-line, and then was away on the scent of the adult deer, almost dragging the gamekeeper in her eagerness. Presently she came to the place where the buck and doe had gone their different ways, and was confronted with a choice. Perhaps one scent lay stronger than the other, perhaps there was a little shift in the wind, perhaps it was pure chance, but she swung right-handed to follow the buck.

When at last the doe reached the grove, she stopped and stood stock-still, listening. In her agitation she was not at first aware of the strange atmosphere of this place that she rarely visited, nor did she notice the figure that sat in the flat spreading boughs of the mighty tree beneath

which she stood. So the sudden sound of a reso-
nant voice above her made her jump four-footed,
and set her heart thumping even more wildly.

'Don't be afraid,' said the voice.

The little roe looked quickly up into the
branches and as quickly down again at sight of
the great strange bird with the blazing eyes. She
paused, half geared to further running, half lulled
to stay a little under the cedar where, curiously,
she suddenly felt a trifle safer.

'Are you the one', she said hesitantly, 'that
they call the Skymaster?'

'I am. What is the matter, sister?'

'They are hunting us,' panted the doe. 'The
man . . . the dog . . . hunting my mate . . . my
children . . . revenge . . . they want revenge.'

'For what? What is it you have done?'

'We stole. From the garden.'

'You stole from the garden, sister?' said the
Skymaster, and his voice was warm with amusement. 'What fruit did you pluck?'

'It wasn't fruit,' said the doe, puzzled. 'It was
Brussels sprouts.'

The Skymaster made a noise that sounded
like a chuckle, and then floated out of the cedar
to stand beside the roe deer, his head a little above
the level of hers, so that from the corner of her

eye she could see the curve of his great bill. She trembled, but held her ground. 'What shall I do?' she said helplessly.

'Go to your children,' said the Skymaster. 'Soon they will have need of you,' and she cantered away through the grove, beneath the tall sequoias and the dark deodars. Hardly had her white-patched rump disappeared from sight than the Skymaster heard in the distance the crack of a rifle.

'Now, they have need of her now,' he said sadly, and he spread his wings and flew towards the sound.

As he followed the spaniel on the trail of the roe buck, the gamekeeper put himself, as the best of huntsmen do, into the position of his quarry. He knew, by the occasional slot-marks in soft places, that however many roe had raided his garden, the hunt had narrowed to one. He checked the eager dog, and sat on a stump to think.

There were several things, he reasoned, that the deer, buck or doe – he knew not which – could now do. It could lie up in cover and hope to remain undetected, it could circle back into the heart of the wood, or it could make for open country.

He did not think it would do any of these things. He thought, he felt sure in fact, that it was making for the stream, and for a good reason. It was planning to use it to throw the dog off the scent, not simply by crossing the stream – it would be an easy matter to cast over the further bank and pick up the line again – but by making its way along the course of it, walking in the shallows, swimming through the pools, using the water to break that invisible thread that bound it to the nose of the dog on land. But would it go upstream or down? He tested the wind with a wetted finger. From the south. And the stream ran roughly north to south. So – upstream, hoping to pass them unseen while they were still among the trees and out of sight of the water.

The gamekeeper stood up, untied the cord from the dog's collar, and sent her on with gesture and quiet encouraging voice. Once the spaniel had gone, he turned and made for the stream.

The minutes passed, and down by the water there was no sound except its own gentle song, no movement but its own lap and ripple in the shoals, its own swirl and eddy in the pools.

Suddenly, around a little bend, the roe buck appeared, treading delicately along a stretch of shallows. He moved without haste, in the very centre of the stream, stopping every now and then to listen and to look towards the flanking wood.

At the end of the gravelly shelf, where the buck walked hock-deep, the stream-bed fell away into a deep pool, and into this he plunged and swam strongly, only his antlered head showing above the surface. At the tail of the pool, quite near to an old hollow-bodied willow whose branches leaned down to trail in the stream, his feet touched bottom again, and he was in the act of shaking water from his coat when the bullet hit him.

The roe fell on his side with a splash, and the gamekeeper, propping his rifle against the trunk of the willow, waded in to grab him by a hind leg and so lug him to the bank. He took out his bone-handled knife and was bending to cut the slender throat when suddenly, with his last strength, the little buck swung his head and lunged at the outstretched arm.

One antler struck the knife and sent it spinning into the water, while the top point of the other ripped across the gamekeeper's hand. Then the roe buck dropped his head and gave a small sigh and died.

Cursing, the gamekeeper looked at his

bleeding hand. The razor-sharp tine had sheared deep across the bottom of the lowest joint of one finger, severing the tendon and slicing through the flexor muscles, rendering it impotent, unbendable, a useless appendage. It was the index finger of his right hand. His trigger finger.

The Skymaster came gliding along the course of the stream until he saw the two figures on the bank ahead. The roe buck lay on his side, head hanging down towards the water, tongue lolling, as though he were longing for a last drink. The gamekeeper sat beside the body, trying to staunch his own wound with a dirty hand-kerchief. The bright blood that still ran from his hand dripped upon the grass to mingle with the dark, congealing gore of the deer. For the buck there was no more pain, but for the other, plenty, and he groaned in its grip, unaware of the silent witness who sat now in the willow tree.

The Skymaster watched as the man got to his feet and stumbled into the stream, peering into the water in quest of his knife, vainly, for it lay now deep at the bottom of the pool. Swearing, he waded back out again, and, pulling out his shirt-tail, tried to rip it to make a bandage, vainly again, for the material was too strong to tear one-handed.

Furious at his inability to help himself, the gamekeeper aimed a vicious kick into the belly of the roe buck, and this action in turn served to remind him of his rifle, left leaning against the tree. Whether or not he had yet made the mental connection between the nature of his injury and the nature of his calling; realized, that is, that neither rifle nor, for that matter, shotgun would ever again be their old deadly selves in his hands, the gamekeeper felt, as always, instinctively uncomfortable when parted from his weapon, and he turned and moved towards the willow to retrieve it.

As he did so, the Skymaster dropped to the ground, knocked down the propped rifle with one buffet of a wing, and stood upon it, grasping it at the point of balance in his talons.

The gamekeeper stopped in his tracks. His long jaw jutted, and he showed his teeth and snarled like a wolf at the sight. A bird, standing on his rifle! And such a bird as he had never seen before...or had he...? Wait...when he was after that jay, something, something big and powerful, had actually knocked his hat off ... he'd caught a glimpse of it among the trees as he'd fired the second barrel ... winged it perhaps, he wasn't sure. Yes, this must be it! And standing on his rifle!

Forgetting the pain in his hand, he ran forward, shouting furiously. He covered perhaps ten of the twenty paces that separated them, all the while expecting the creature to fly away. But it made no movement except to half-spread its wings, whose span, the gamekeeper could see, looked to be very large. The bird had, he suddenly saw, an air of great ferocity, and the talons that grasped the rifle were fearsome. He stopped and looked around. Finding a convenient stout stick, he picked it up in his left hand.

Now they looked directly into each other's eyes, one pair cold ice-blue, one pair hot sun-orange, and neither dropped his gaze.

For a long, long moment the man and the bird stared at one another, and then the dog ran yapping out of the wood, and the tableau dissolved into movement.

Simultaneously the man came on, raising his stick, and the bird beat his great wings and rose into the air, out of reach of the blow, and sailed out over the stream, over the pool, over the deepest part of the pool. He carried the rifle gripped in his claws as easily as though it had been a bulrush, while the man shouted and the dog barked. And over the deepest part of the pool, he dropped it, and hovered over the water to watch it sink, to rest and rust beside the bone-handled knife.

Then the Skymaster dived once, in salute, over the body of the roe buck, and flew away into Godhanger.

CHAPTER SIX

The night of All Saints' Day brought the first frost of winter to Godhanger Wood. A full moon shone down on the gamekeeper's cottage. Inside it, the man slept fitfully. Not yet fully understanding the seriousness of his injury, he had not sought help from the world outside. In the wood he had been wounded, and in the wood, in due time, the wound would heal. He had strapped the useless dangling index finger of his right hand to its neighbour with sticking plaster, but the pain of the injury continually woke him, and once awake his anger boiled up again.

He cursed the roe buck, whose gralloched carcase now hung head down in his larder, but principally he cursed the great bird which, for the second time in a short while, had challenged his authority and set itself against him, in his wood, in Godhanger.

'I'll kill that bloody bird if it's the last thing I

do!' he swore again and again as he tossed and turned.

Outside the cottage his spaniel kicked and twitched in a hunting dream as she lay in the straw of her kennel, while from the henhouse at the far side of the garden came occasional sleepy murmurs and chuckles from the birds dozing upon their perches.

In the long strip of the gamekeeper's garden, there was movement under the moon. As well as the odd rat making its way down from midden to henhouse, there were woodmice flitting among the stalks of the ruined Brussels sprouts, and in a cabbage patch Odden the pigmy shrew ran frantically about. He was searching for the snails, slugs, worms and beetles that were needed to satisfy his voracious appetite. Though weighing only 150 grams, smallest of all the country's mammals, Odden could eat four times his own weight in a day and a half. Indeed to go without food for more than a few hours meant death, so that for the pigmy shrew, life was one unending hunt.

The midden itself looked to be alive, its surface a skin of constant movement as Rawden and his tribe crawled about it, feasting upon and dragging away the bowels of the slain roe buck. Sharp squeaks broke the silence as they squabbled over the guts, and sharp ears heard the noise.

Glyde the tawny owl came floating through the trees and pitched on a branch of the walnut. He was normally the noisiest of his tribe, beginning each dusk with his sharp call of 'E-wick!' and continuing to hoot throughout the night.

But now he sat silent, head cocked, black eyes staring.

Glyde's were not the only eyes watching the rat feast. Upwind, behind the broken pigsty wall, Flem and Fitz crouched. Like foxes everywhere they were partial to fat rat, and they remembered the size of the one which Gilbert the wild cat had caught on the night of his death. Now only Gilbert's bones lay strewn about the refuse-heap, for the rats had eaten him and the ants had cleaned up afterwards. Grotesquely, the moonlight shone through the empty eye-sockets of his skull.

As the foxes tensed themselves for a sudden joint leap over the low wall, Glyde dropped noiselessly out of the walnut tree and fastened upon a young rat, gripping it tightly in the three talons of one foot. The rat shrieked, the rest of the colony vanished, and as the foxes came over the wall, the tawny owl lifted away with his prey.

They leaped at him and fell back, cursing.

'Bloody owl!' snarled Flem and Fitz with one voice.

They sniffed about the surface of the midden, but the rats had eaten the best of the deer guts, and now the wind brought a whiff of a much more appetizing scent from the henhouse.

'Let us go down, brother,' said Flem. 'Oh, what I could do to a fat chicken!'

'Wait a while, brother,' said Fitz. 'Remember the gun. Remember the cat.'

They waited, eyes, ears, noses at full alert for some minutes, and then they padded side by side down the garden strip.

Seeing a movement, Fitz pounced. Between his forepaws was a tiny body.

'What have you there?' asked Flem.

'It is but a mouthful,' answered Fitz, and he lowered his muzzle to snap up the pygmy shrew.

But Odden, like all his kind, bore upon each flank a gland that could emit a foul musky smell, and now, with a thin high squeal, he released this secret weapon.

'Faugh!' spat Fitz, recoiling in disgust, while Odden bounded away in a series of minute hops.

'What a stink!' said Flem, nose wrinkling.

Foxes are quick to learn, and neither of the

two young brothers would bother with shrews again, each assured the other.

Drawn by the hen-smell, they moved on slowly, very cautiously. The scent of dog was strong too, and though they did not know that the animal was chained, they had no wish for this preliminary reconnaissance to be interrupted by a volley of barking.

Partly because of the instincts of their race, partly because of their brotherhood, Flem and Fitz each knew that they were unlikely to eat chicken that night. All they wanted was a good look round the place, an investigation, to see if there were any weaknesses in the defences within which the man kept his birds.

Was the wire-netting of the run weak, rusted perhaps, so that it could be breached? And if it were breached, could the pop-hole that gave access to the hens' sleeping quarters be lifted by a paw? And if it could be lifted, was the pop-hole big enough to admit a fox?

But since the answer to the first of these three questions was, they found, 'No', the answers to the others must remain unknown.

They saw something else, however.

At the rear of the henhouse, in a narrow space between the back of the wooden shed and the wall behind it, they found the mouth of a rat-hole, the hole that led into the tunnel up which Rawden crept to steal eggs. It was a big hole, for Rawden was a big rat.

The foxes put their noses to it.

'Suppose, brother,' said Flem, 'that that tunnel runs right underneath?'

'And suppose, brother,' said Fitz, 'that it comes up through the floor of the henhouse?'

'All it needs is a little work. The man would never notice.'

'Until what is now only a rat's tunnel becomes a fox's tunnel.'

'And then what feasting there will be, brother,' said Flem.

'All shall die,' said Fitz.

With the rich scent of chicken in their nostrils and the hens' sleepy murmurings in their ears, the brothers could not resist making a start on their digging.

They took turns, one sitting on guard in the frosty moonlight while the other scrabbled away at the hole, earth flying out behind him.

It was awkward work, for the space was cramped, the wall being so close to the henhouse. But by the time the wistful song of an early robin told of the dawn, they had tunnelled almost a fox length underneath.

As the light strengthened, they slipped away up the garden, pausing on top of the pigsty wall to look back.

'We have made a start,' said Fitz.

'And tomorrow,' said Flem, 'we will make an end. Blood shall be shed.'

'Your blood,' said a voice above them, 'unless you will be warned.'

Startled, the foxes looked up to see, in the branches of the walnut tree, the shadowy shape of a great bird.

Flem and Fitz wrinkled their lips, partly in anger, and partly in fear, for this bird was larger than any they had ever seen in their young lives, and now, in the growing light, they could see the size of its talons and the hook of its big beak.

'Who are you?' they growled.

'A friend,' said the Skymaster quietly. 'If you will let me be.'

'We don't need friends,' spat Fitz.

'We have each other,' snarled Flem.

'You have each other today,' said the Skymaster. 'But what of the morrow? Think long and hard before you return to your digging, young brothers. You may be digging your own grave. Go back to your earth in the safe depths of

Godhanger and come to this place no more.'

'Why don't you mind your own business?' said Flem.

'You are my business,' replied the Skymaster. 'You and all the other creatures of the wood. I told you, I am your friend.'

'Well, you can stuff your friendship,' said Fitz.

'So be it. I can but warn you.'

'Oh, flap off!' cried the foxes rudely.

For a long moment the great bird stared down, and then he lifted away out of the walnut tree and began to climb, with slow powerful wing-beats, into the lightening sky.

Just before he passed from their sight, the foxes heard his cry; a scream that ended in a yelp.

It was a sad sound.

The gamekeeper rose with the sun.

After so broken a night's sleep, his temper was even viler than usual, particularly as, because of his injury, he must needs become left-handed. Clothes were awkward to button, bootlaces to tie, and he cut himself shaving.

He stumped outside and let the dog off her chain, but when, after squatting to make water, she ran back to him, fawning, he aimed a kick at her.

He took a tin bowl of corn into the hen-run and opened the pop-hole. Then, as he was feeding the birds, he heard the spaniel snuffling and whining in the narrow space between the back of the henhouse and the wall. Rats, thought the gamekeeper and he went to investigate.

A dog's nose is infinitely more sensitive than a man's, but to the gamekeeper also the reek of fox was unmistakable, and though the gap was too narrow for him to get in, he could see the size of the hole and the heap of spoil from the night's digging.

He cast about on the rough greenish patch that served as a lawn, and there, clear in the frosted grass, were two sets of fox footprints.

'Bastards!' growled the gamekeeper. 'I'll fill you full of lead.'

He imagined the scene that coming night – the two foxes trotting down the garden in the bright moonlight, himself in hiding, and then the double report, a right and left, and two limp corpses to hang upon the gibbet.

After he had eaten some breakfast, the gamekeeper took down his gun from its place on the wall. Only then, handling it, did he fully realize what a blow the roe buck had struck in its death-throes. Not only was his trigger finger useless but, now that it was strapped to its neighbour, the two fingers together were too thick and clumsy to get within the trigger-guard.

He took off the plaster and tried reaching the trigger with his middle finger only, but the injured one got in the way and he hurt himself.

There was only one thing for it. He must teach himself to shoot left-handed. He must throw the stock into his left shoulder, support the barrels with his right hand, pull the trigger with his left index finger. It would not be easy to break the habits of a lifetime. For one thing, the stock was the wrong shape, not built for a left-hander. He would be slower, less accurate.

Better if he still had his rifle, and time to draw a bead upon a stationary target. But his rifle lay rusting at the bottom of the pool, thanks to that bloody bird!

Yes, he would kill the foxes, and, once he had learned to shoot left-handed, many other creatures in Godhanger Wood that he classed as vermin. Crows, magpies, jays, owls, hawks – all would hang upon the gibbet. But above all, the gamekeeper longed to see one great spread-eagled body nailed to the wooden crossbar.

Now, disregarding the pain of his wound, he buckled on his cartridge-belt, slung his game-bag over his shoulder, and set out into the wood, his dog at heel, his gun in the crook of his left arm.

In the cedar of Lebanon, in the centre of that strange grove of exotic trees, four of the followers of the Skymaster sat waiting.

'He is late,' said Glyde the tawny owl sonorously. 'It is long past sun-up. What can have delayed him?'

'He's having a lie-in, I expect,' said the little owl Eustace.

'A lie-in?' said Glyde in shocked tones. 'The Skymaster does not indulge in such slothful behaviour. He is ever busy on our behalf. His work is never done.'

'So he gets tired,' said Eustace. 'Stands to reason. He's only avian, you know.'

'Caar!' said Darcy the carrion crow in a disapproving voice. 'You should have more respect for the Master.'

'Surely you should know by now, my good Eustace,' said Glyde in his pompous way, 'that he is different from the rest of us?'

'Yes,' said Eustace. 'Bigger.'

'Little owl, little sense,' said Darcy.

Just then Myles, perched high in the cedar as usual, began to chatter. 'He comes, he comes!' the magpie called, and seconds later they heard the 'whoosh' of great wings braking to a stop, and then the Skymaster was amongst them once more, while the big spreading branch upon which he had pitched swayed down beneath his weight and then rose again.

'Good morrow, Master,' said Glyde. 'We knew that you would come, even though it is later than usual,' and, despite himself, he yawned.

'Get you to your roost, old night-hunter,' said the Skymaster, 'before the little birds of the day come to mob and tease you. Darcy and Myles and Eustace will tell you later what I have to say.'

'But, Master . . .' began Glyde.

'No buts. Begone.'

'Cu-cu-cu!' cried Eustace harshly. As always when excited, he clicked his beak and bobbed his head up and down at the sight of Glyde's silent departure.

'You shut the old windbag up all right, Master!' he said.

'Keep silent, little one,' said the Skymaster evenly. 'And Myles, come down, and Darcy, come closer.' When they had all obeyed, he said, 'Listen, my friends, for I have work for you today.'

Then he told them of the death of the roe buck and of the wounding of the gamekeeper.

'He is abroad in the wood now,' he said, 'with murder in his heart.'

'Is it not always in his heart, Master?' said Darcy mournfully.

'Yes. But this day he comes to kill anything and everything that crosses his path. Today his bitterness, his malice, his cruelty are such as Godhanger has never yet seen.'

At that moment they heard a distant shot, and then another.

'Two dead,' said Eustace.

'Not so,' said the Skymaster. 'He missed.'

'How do you . . . ?' began Eustace, and then he shut his beak abruptly.

'He missed', said the Skymaster, 'because now he has to shoot in a different manner. So he needs to practise, and that is why there is danger today not just to what he calls vermin, but to everything that moves, to the small, to the weak, to the innocent. Fly out now, the three of you, and spread the alarm about the wood. Fly first to your mates and tell them, and then pass the word to all that fly by day, to the sparrowhawks and the kestrels and the buzzards, to the jackdaws and the jays, to the pigeons and the doves and the song-birds and even to the sparrows, lest they fall before him. Warn all, and tell those that can to spread that warning, each in his own fashion. Go now.'

As they flew out, a third shot sounded.

When the wood pigeon had suddenly come clattering out of an oak tree, the gamekeeper had had to throw up his gun in what was for him a cack-handed way, its butt into his left shoulder.

Normally, that pigeon would never have eaten another acorn, but as it was, the pattern of shot flew well wide of it, and by the time the man fired the choke barrel the bird was out of range.

As the gamekeeper ejected the spent cartridges and reloaded, he heard a thin familiar trilling from a nearby bush. Friendly and fearless, the robin sang his sad song.

Taking his time, the gamekeeper set himself into the unaccustomed firing position and looked carefully along the barrels at the small unmoving target. As the blast ripped into the bush, the spaniel ran forward, tail feathering, and picked up what little was left of the redbreast.

'Drop it!' snapped the gamekeeper, and moved on into the depths of the wood, alert for more target practice.

But all of a sudden the silence that had fallen after the crash of the shot was broken, first by one voice and then by more and more in a growing chorus, as the birds of Godhanger Wood received and reacted to the Skymaster's bidding.

Before long the air was filled with alarm-calls – the chatter of magpies, the cawing of crows, the high-pitched cries of jackdaws, the mewing of buzzards, the cackling of blackbirds, and, loudest of all, the screech of the widowed jay.

'Skraaark!' she screamed. 'The murderer's about! Beware! Beware!'

Never before had there been such tumult in Godhanger. Never before had the gamekeeper heard such a cacophony of sound in the wood. Gun at the ready, he peered about, into the bramble-brakes and thickets, and up into the leafless trees. But there was never a bird to be seen. He could hear their cries everywhere, was almost deafened by them as the great chorus followed him about, but set eyes on them he could not, and, maddened, he began to loose off shots at random. But to no avail. Not until he had given up and begun to stump furiously back towards his cottage did the clamour die away.

In the renewed stillness, the gamekeeper heard, as he entered his garden, the shout of one of his hens, celebrating the laying of an egg, and this reminded him of the foxes.

His ice-blue eyes narrowed, and he swore to himself that they should die, that night, when they returned to their tunnelling. Much of his old skill with the shotgun might have gone, but he could still hit a sitting robin. Or a digging fox.

Loftus the raven came floating over from the sea-cliffs towards the combe on whose flank lay Godhanger. Below him, the intervening fields were white with frost.

Then suddenly, as he crossed the hog-mane of the wood's horsehead shape, he heard the sound of a thousand alarm-calls from birds of every sort, and then, after a while, the banging of gunshots.

Loftus circled, high above the wood, until, just as abruptly, the bird cries died away and at the same time he could see, far below, the figure of a man come out of the trees into the eye of the horsehead. The old raven planed down towards the lowest point of the horse's neck, where, now that the hardwood trees were leafless, the dark shapes of those in the grove stood out clearly.

Emboldened by the knowledge that the gamekeeper had returned to his cottage, Loftus dropped lower, impelled, he knew not why, towards the greatest among the strange foreign trees.

Then from the depths of the cedar of Lebanon came a now familiar voice, calling his name. Landing among the branches, the raven once more found that here, try as he would, he could not bring himself to look directly upon the great bird who stared unblinkingly at him.

'Master,' he said, 'what was all that noise about? Never in my long life have I heard such a racket in Godhanger. Every bird in the wood was calling, it seemed.'

'Every bird in the wood,' said the Skymaster, 'was at risk this morning. Now, together, they have driven off the evil one, for the moment. But not for long. More blood will be shed, this coming night.'

'Who dies?' asked Loftus.

'One who is not old and wise as you are,' said the Skymaster, 'but young and foolish. As we all were, once.'

'You?' said Loftus. 'Foolish?'

The Skymaster made a noise that sounded like a chuckle. 'I have played the fool in my time,' he said. 'Though I suspect you think of me as a sobersides.'

'Well . . .' began the raven, preparing to deny this.

'You see me as a pompous creature, don't you? A bit of a prig, eh?'

Loftus said nothing.

'Your silence is your answer, I fear.'

'No,' said Loftus after a while. 'I heard Eustace say once that you had a sense of humour and I will confess that I doubted it. But now that I know you better, I believe it to be so. I believe you are laughing at me now, Master. Maybe it is I who am the pompous prig.'

'I do not laugh at you, Loftus,' said the Skymaster, 'but I hope to laugh with you, if there is time.'

'Time?'

'For us to fly together, in happy companion-ship, as we have once done. I shall not easily for-get that carefree jesting display of yours, when you flew with all the joy and abandon of a youngster. Who knows, maybe you will teach me to turn somersaults in the air! But now get you back to your cliff-ledge, Loftus, to your mate, and to the safety that is not to be found in Godhanger. Here, not many live long lives.'

'But you will, Master,' said Loftus in his deep voice. 'Surely you will live for . . . ?' And then he stopped.

'. . . for ever,' answered the other.

'I cannot understand,' croaked the raven.

'You will. One day you will, Loftus. Your eyes, my friend, shall be the last to see me.'

'What did he mean, do you suppose?' said Loftus later to his slightly smaller mate.

They were sitting side by side on their ledge below the cliff-top, this old married couple (for they had been together three score years and ten), and now and then they touched beaks companionably.

For answer the hen raven made a noise that sounded like the popping of a cork from a bottle, which meant, Loftus knew, 'I couldn't tell you, I'm sure.'

'What did he mean,' he said again, 'that I should be the last to see him? I still cannot look him in the eye.'

'Why not? Are you afraid of this "Master" of yours?'

'Of him?' said Loftus. 'No. *For* him, yes. Godhanger Wood is a place of death. How fortunate we are, my dear, to live here, on the high cliffs, in the salt winds, above the ceaseless swell of the ocean,' and he jumped off the ledge and let the upsurge of air that ran up the cliff face lift him high into the clear skies.

'Prrruk!' the hen raven heard him call in that

deep voice. 'Prrruk! Prrruk!' which meant, she knew, 'I am free. I am strong. I am the greatest of the crows.'

Back in Godhanger, the birds of the day went about their business as usual. Jeb the jackdaw and his mate sat, just out of gunshot range, in the walnut tree at the top of the gamekeeper's garden, ready to give warning when next he should emerge from his cottage.

As for the animals of the night, they slept the hours of light away.

In his nest in a stickpile, Rippin the polecat lay curled, twitching once in a while in blood-thirsty dreams.

Deep in the badger sett that lay roughly in the middle of Godhanger, in the thick of the horse's neck, as it were, Baldwin and his tribe slept soundly. Built into a mound or tump of ground on which grew a scatter of elder trees, their trunks marked by long scratches where the badgers stood up to clean their claws, the great sett had twenty or so different entrances, and within it there were a large number of chambers on different levels.

A disused chamber on the fringe of the sett had been occupied as their earth by the two young foxes, Flem and Fitz. The badgers did not seem to object to these lodgers, but the foxes steered respectfully clear of their landlords, should they meet, especially of the great boar, Baldwin. Flem and Fitz slumbered peacefully, though occasionally one or other would kick out as he dreamt of the tunnel beneath the henhouse and of the killing to come.

Meanwhile the jackdaws in the walnut had tired of their sentry-go. Not daring to search for snails and slugs in the gamekeeper's garden while the man was at home, they had flown away into the wood to look for acorns.

No one saw the gamekeeper come out later, carrying an odd-shaped steel object in his left hand. He went to the back of the henhouse, to the narrow space between it and the wall, and knelt down. Slowly, because of his injury, and very carefully, he set a trap in the mouth of the unfinished tunnel, concealing it afterwards with a scatter of dead leaves. As he got to his feet, his dog came forward to investigate, only to be cursed and then, for its own safety, chained up.

The gamekeeper was not only angry but confused. What was happening in his wood? That great clamour of alarm-calls that had followed him wherever he went, pestering him, mocking him, it seemed – such a thing had never happened before. What could have caused the birds of Godhanger to unite against him in that way? Was it somehow to do with that bloody bird that had picked up his precious rifle in its talons and dropped it into the river? If that damned roe buck had not slashed him, he could still have relied on his trusty shotgun. But now even that was no longer the weapon it had been.

Once he had been the finest of shots, supremely confident in his skill; able cleanly to kill any bird that flew – the high pheasant, the whirring partridge, the jinking snipe, the elusive woodcock roding in and out among the trees. And now what was he reduced to? Hitting a sitting robin at close range.

If the foxes come tonight, he thought, I'm as likely as not to miss. What's more, the weather's on the change, the moon may well be clouded over, and I can smell rain. Damned if I'll sit out in the dark and the wet half the night when they may not come anyway, and I need sleep. Thus it was that he had decided to set the steel gin-trap with its cruel serrated jaws.

First, he had hung it over his fire, for the smoke to mask his own scent. Then he had worn gloves, to set it. Attached to the gin was a length of chain ending in a metal peg which the game-keeper hammered into the ground. Once caught, there would be no escape by dragging the trap away.

'Half a loaf', said the gamekeeper to his spaniel as he chained her in her kennel, 'is better than no bread. I'll have one of the devils, anyway.'

The gamekeeper had been right about the weather. In the late afternoon the wind backed westerly, the sky clouded over, and a shower fell. At dusk the foxes came out of their earth, yawning and stretching, and then, because they were young and needed still to play, they began a game of tag over and around the badgers' sett. First Flem would chase Fitz as he dodged and doubled among the elder trees, and then vice versa.

They ceased their game abruptly as Baldwin stuck his broad striped head out of one of the entry holes and then emerged, followed by a number of half-grown cubs. As the foxes trotted away, they heard behind them a loud noise of clucking and chattering as Baldwin's children began to enjoy their own evening rough-and-tumble.

'To our digging then, brother,' said Flem.

'Blood shall be spilled, brother,' said Fitz.

As before, they paused when they reached

the broken pigsty wall, and, as before, Fitz advised caution. But Flem, the more headstrong of the two, trotted straight down the strip of garden, his nostrils filled with hen-smell, and without pausing slipped into the narrow gap by the wall.

Fitz, following, heard a sudden metallic snap, and then a shrill yelp of pain, whereupon the dog began to bark loudly.

'Help me, brother; I am held by the leg!' gasped Flem, but next moment there came the sound of a door opening, and Fitz, seeing a dark figure emerging, fled.

By the pigsty wall he paused, hearing his brother give one last despairing yap. Then came the sound of a dull thumping thud. The gamekeeper was not one to waste a cartridge when a good bash on the head with a heavy club would do.

As Fitz melted away, so a few great drops of rain fell, like tears.

## CHAPTER SEVEN

The rain went on through the night, and the next day dawned bright and fresh and clean, with a cloudless pale blue sky. It was the kind of peerless weather sometimes to be found in that handover time between autumn and winter, and Godhanger Wood lay clean-washed on the side of the combe, seeming to be a place of perfect peace and quiet.

Eustace the little owl stood in his doorway, a knothole in the trunk of an old ash, and listened to the small sounds around him. As with all owls, one ear was positioned slightly higher than the other, allowing him to listen both up and down. He yawned, feeling sleepy, and half decided that he could not be bothered to fly to the grove, to the cedar, to the morning gathering.

Just then he heard a loud harsh voice further up the slope, and before long the hen jay came flying past. 'Dead fox!' she screeched. 'Dead fox! Skraark!'

Eustace, curiosity aroused, took off from the mouth of his hole. He well knew where many of those that died in the wood ended up. His swooping, erratic, batlike flight was not suited to lengthy journeys, and he stopped two or three times to perch and look around for safety's sake, before he reached the place where the gibbet stood.

This was in a little clearing not far from the ruined pigsty, and the gibbet itself was a T-shape, consisting of a stout post driven into the ground, across the top of which was fixed, at a height of about a metre and a half, a long wooden plank.

Eustace landed in the walnut tree on the far side from the gamekeeper's cottage, and looked down. Most of the corpses fixed to the plank were old and partly mummified – the cock jay, some stoats, a squirrel – but in the centre of the gibbet, nailed by its brush to the top of the post, hung the tawny body of Flem, open-mouthed, the white teeth showing in a last desperate snarl.

Then, with his lower ear, Eustace heard the cottage door open and the man's voice and the dog whining to be loosed from its chain, and he flew hastily away again, in the direction of the grove.

I think I'll go to the gathering after all, he said to himself. The rest may have heard the news, but they won't have actually seen the body, like me. Trapped, that fox had been, by the look of one leg, and then smacked on the head. Ah well, that's life. Or rather, death.

When the little owl did eventually arrive at the cedar of Lebanon, he found it filled with birds. The Skymaster was there, of course, in the midst of them, and amongst them Eustace saw, to his great surprise, the big black shape of the old raven Loftus.

Good job I came, thought the little owl. I should have been the only absentee of the twelve followers of the Skymaster.

He swivelled his round head to look at the other eleven, and then he spoke to the one at whom he dared not look.

'Sorry I'm late, Master,' he said. 'You will know where I've been.'

'I do,' said the Skymaster.

'The fox is on the gibbet,' said Eustace to the rest.

At this, the buzzards gave their usual mournful cry, and Glyde, never averse to making a speech, especially on sad occasions, declaimed, 'Alas, poor creature! Cut down in the first flower of its youth and beauty!'

'He's not cut down, he's hung up,' said Eustace, 'and it's a flipping fox we're talking about, Glyde, an animal that would have made short work of you or any of us, if he could have caught us in the first flower of his youth and beauty. Foxes are killers.'

'So are owls,' said the Skymaster. 'And hawks and falcons and the crow family. All of you are killers.'

There was a short silence, and then said deep-voiced Loftus, 'And you, Master?'

'I must eat,' said the Skymaster. 'Like you.'

'So must the man,' said Eustace. 'He needs meat.'

'Of the roe deer, yes. Of pigeon or pheasant or partridge, or rabbit or hare, yes. Like us, he kills to eat. But unlike us, he kills also for killing's sake, a jaybird, a robin, a fox. Man is the one true murderer.'

'It has always been so,' said Glyde sepulchrally. 'It will always be so.'

Eustace rocked back and forth, clattering his beak. 'Cu-cu-cu!' he cried. 'What a little ray of sunshine you are, Glyde, always looking on the bright side. If ever I finish upon the gibbet, I just hope I'm not hanging next to you. That would be a fate worse than death.'

At that moment, Myles, who was as ever perched in the top of the cedar of Lebanon, cried, 'Man coming!'

Within seconds the tree was empty of birds, save two. The Skymaster still sat unmoving, and at his side, fearful yet somehow unwilling to leave, sat Loftus.

The gamekeeper seldom entered the grove. Though part of his wood, there was something about this stand of exotic trees – the great cedar, the deodars, the cypresses, the tall wellingtonias and the monkey puzzles with their stiff spine-tipped leaves – that repelled him. Their very foreignness made him uncomfortable.

But this morning he had decided to walk through it – hoping for some left-handed shooting practice – when from the greatest of the trees he suddenly saw a number of birds fly out; birds, he noted, of several different kinds, that he would not have expected to be consorting.

He moved forward, dog at heel, gun at the ready, and Loftus, seeing him coming, was filled with fear.

'Don't be afraid,' said the Skymaster softly, and at that precise moment the dog put up a rabbit out of the undergrowth, which scuttled away in the opposite direction.

Wheeling, the gamekeeper fired and missed, and fired the second barrel, not killing the animal cleanly as of old but hitting it somewhere far back, as its squealing told him. As it tried to drag itself away, he sent the spaniel after it, and followed to give the *coup de grâce*.

'See,' said the Skymaster. 'He did not come, Loftus. You were safe with me.'

'But, Master,' began the raven, and then stopped.

'Well?'

'Will you always be here, here in Godhanger?'

'For ever and ever.'


Rippin was the last of his kind in Godhanger, the last indeed anywhere in that countryside.

Polecats are killers of anything they come upon – rabbits, rats, mice, birds, frogs, snakes – and, if they get the chance, of poultry. The size of the victim is no deterrent to them, so that not only hens but geese and turkeys too are fair game; and because poultry belong to man, man kills the polecat.

Rippin's mate and all their children had, over time, died at the hands of the gamekeeper, by gun or trap or poison, and now he was the sole survivor of his race.

After dark he snaked his way out of his stick-pile to begin his night's hunting. At about the same time, the gamekeeper was sitting down to a meal of roast rabbit, while the dog sat at his feet, hoping for scraps, and, on the midden, Rawden and the other rats squabbled over the last of the rabbit's paunch and guts.

The polecat made his sinuous way through the blackness of the wood, alert for scents of ground-nesting or low-perching birds. Rippin's own scent was very strong and acrid, and creatures that winded him crouched rigid with terror, as the foumart, or foul marten, passed by.

That night he was making for the game-keeper's cottage.

Like the foxes, he too longed above all things to kill those fat sleepy muttering hens. Then he would drink their blood. Many times before he had prowled around the henhouse, looking for a way in and finding none. Lack of success did not make him less hopeful that one night, somehow, he would be lucky.

Warned by his rank odour, the rats were already deep inside their midden fortress as Rippin slithered over the pigsty wall and ran, in long, low jumps, down the strip of the garden.

At the back of the henhouse he smelled a mixture of man and fox and dog, and then he saw what he had never seen before – a large fresh-dug hole in the space by the wall. He dived into this hole and rippled along a metre of tunnel, before it became too narrow for him. For though the original tunneller, Rawden, was a giant among rats, Rippin was more than twice his size.

Normally polecats are not great diggers, preferring to live in burrows ready-made by rabbits, or in rock crevices, or in a pile of sticks like Rippin's present home, but now, maddened by the overpowering smell of chicken just above his head, he began to scratch and scrape madly, to enlarge the rest of the rat runway.

In the space of half an hour he had scrabbled onwards and upwards until the tip of his snout emerged through the exit hole in the old floorboards of the henhouse, the hole from which Rawden had crept out to steal eggs. It was but the work of moments for Rippin's sharp teeth to bite away a few extra centimetres of wood softened by many years' coating of droppings, and then he was in.

The gamekeeper had just finished his meal and thrown a bit of meat to his dog when, as he was wiping round his plate with a piece of bread, he heard a sudden outburst of noise from his hen-house, a frantic chorus of squawks and shrieks.

The other fox, he thought, and, cursing because his injury slowed him, he took down his gun and loaded it, kicked off slippers and pulled on boots, and, grabbing a torch, hurried outside, the barking dog running before him.

The door of the henhouse was on the far side from the cottage and beside it was a small single-paned window. Shining his torch through this, the gamekeeper saw a stark sight.

Scattered about the floor, some dead and already still, some yet twitching and jumping in their death throes, were eleven of his twelve old hens. Crouched above the twelfth was the pole-cat.

So carried away was Rippin by his blood lust that, as the light shone on him, he paused to spit and hiss at it, catlike, before sinking his teeth into the scrawny neck of the last bird.

Handicapped though he was, the game-keeper acted fast. Memorizing the spot where the polecat was crouching, he dropped the torch, pushed the muzzle of his gun straight through the glass of the window, and, at a range of no more than a metre or so, loosed off both barrels.

Rippin the blood-drinker, the merciless, the

foul-smelling, the last of the polecats, was blown into rags.

Next morning no jay came screeching about a dead polecat or twelve dead hens, for though many had heard the gunfire in the night, no one was aware of the massacre in the henhouse.

Only the four most regular followers, Glyde, Darcy, Myles and Eustace, attended the early morning gathering in the cedar, and all were puzzled by something the Skymaster said.

The weather had turned colder again, and Eustace was complaining about it, fluffing out his feathers. 'Roll on next summer and a bit of warmth,' he said, to which the Skymaster replied, 'There is plenty of heat in a funeral pyre.'

It was the buzzards who first noticed the rising column of smoke. Dropping lower from their pitches high above Godhanger, they could see the blaze, right in the eye of the horsehead, that was causing the smoke, and they circled above with mournful cries of 'Peee-ooo!'

The gamekeeper had decided upon the only fitting end for his hens as he sat eating the last of their eggs for breakfast.

He would not eat the birds – not only would the scraggy old things be as tough as leather but the bodies stank of the musky reek of the polecat

– and their ramshackle house was not worth repairing. He would burn it, and all of them and the remains of their assassin within it. He pulled out the dry dusty straw from their nest boxes, heaping it in the middle of the floor, added a number of torn-up paper meal-sacks, broke up the perches and laid them on top of the bonfire, and then lit it.

As he stood, lantern jaw jutting, ice-blue eyes narrowed, and watched the old henhouse blazing, so his anger blazed up again, anger against all the creatures of Godhanger, especially the roe buck, the fox, the polecat, and above all, against that bird, that great nameless bird. He looked up the garden towards the walnut tree, beyond which stood the gibbet. He shall hang there, he swore to himself, if it's the last thing I do.

Loftus, sailing above the cliff-top fields in search of carrion, saw in the distance the column of smoke and made his way across to investigate. Seeing the buzzards circling, the raven toyed with the thought of a bit of teasing. Master of the air, he had always enjoyed upsetting the big hawks, so slow and clumsy by comparison. But something, he knew not what, decided him against the idea, and he left them alone. All the same, the big hawks, seeing him, departed, moaning to one another that the raven never gave them a moment's peace.

As he watched them go, Loftus suddenly heard, high above him, a shrill yelping cry, and, rolling hastily on to his back, saw the majestic outline of the Skymaster. He climbed to meet him.

'Master, you called?' he croaked.

'But to greet you, Loftus,' was the reply. 'Come, fly with me a little,' and side by side the greatest of the crows and the greatest of all the birds circled above the smoking ruins of the gamekeeper's henhouse.

'What burns?' asked Loftus.

'A pyre,' said the Skymaster. 'Last night there was much killing. Twelve innocents died and a murderer was murdered. Now all are consumed by fire, save he who most deserves to die.'

Though Loftus had not noticed, they had, while speaking, been gradually losing height.

Now suddenly he realized that they were no more than a hundred metres above the clearing in which stood the cottage and in which the remnants of the burned henhouse still smoked, and, looking down, he saw the man staring up at them. He saw him shake a fist and hurry indoors, and then re-emerge, hastily loading his gun.

Still the Skymaster circled calmly, great

wings outspread as though in blessing. The raven
heard him say, once again, 'Don't be afraid,
Loftus,' and, strangely, he was not.

He saw the barrels foreshorten as the gun
was pointed skywards, and then came the double
crash of the shots. An instant later Loftus felt the
lightest pattering on his black feathering as a few
of the pellets reached him, at extreme range,
harmlessly.

Turning now, the Skymaster swept away over
Godhanger Wood, Loftus following. In his excitement and relief, the raven rolled and curvetted
like the aerial acrobat he was, calling loudly the
while, 'He cannot kill you, Master! The man cannot kill you!'

'Not yet,' came the reply.

'It came to gloat over me,' said the gamekeeper softly to his dog, as he watched the two
birds flying away. The spaniel wagged her tail
madly, delighted at the quiet tones instead of the
usual snapped commands or curses.

'Looking down on me, calm as you please,'
the man went on, 'as much as to say "You can't
kill me". Just let it get within range. I'll blow its
bloody head off.'

As he sat later, cleaning his gun, he made two
resolutions. First, he would somehow turn him-

self into as good a shot as he had once been, even though he must shoot left-handed. Second, he would spend every waking hour hunting that great bird. Ever since it had come, from God knows where, cruel luck had dogged him. Only when he had nailed it to the gibbet would he feel that the wood was once more his.

Now, as winter set in, the gamekeeper prowled through Godhanger Wood from dawn to dusk, shooting at everything that moved.

Rabbits died, and the occasional hare, and a lot of squirrels (for good measure he blasted every one of their dreys that he came across, in case anyone was at home). Many small birds – with whom once the gamekeeper would have had no quarrel and on whom he would certainly have never wasted a cartridge – met their end as victims of his target practice.

Residents like sparrows and starlings and chaffinches and tomtits, and winter visitors such as fieldfares and redwings, tumbled from branch or bush or out of the skies as he honed his skills. Only the gamebirds were sometimes exempted, for even in his madness, his professional instincts stopped him from decimating the stocks of pheasants or the partridge coveys or the silent darting woodcock.

This slaughter went on despite the continued best efforts of the birds of Godhanger to give warning to the unwary. Wherever the man went he was followed always by a chorus of alarm-calls of every sort. Mostly he could only rage at the unseen callers but sometimes one would show itself and pay the penalty. But whereas once he had been able to move silently through the trees, now there was noise over and around and about him, from the moment he stepped out of his door until he returned to close it behind him.

Perhaps because he did not like the place, was in fact in a strange way afraid of it, the game-keeper in his patrolling always came last to the grove. By the time he had combed the rest of Godhanger and its bordering fields, the morning gathering was always over and no birds were to be seen in the cedar of Lebanon or indeed in any of the other great dark conifers. He never tarried there, but always strode quickly through.

So the winter wore on, a mild one at first, but becoming colder, with frequent gales of wind howling in from the west, and, around the turn of the year, a great night-time thunderstorm, seemingly directly above the combe, which was filled with a cannonade of noise and lanced by light-ning bolts.

One of these struck the cedar of Lebanon at the point where one of its great arms joined the trunk. Though torn, the branch did not break away from the tree but hung awkwardly, like a fractured limb. It was in fact the branch upon which the Skymaster always sat at the morning gathering. All knew it to be his, and none ever dared perch there.

He was sitting upon it at daybreak after the thunderstorm, nearer to the ground now than before so that he had to raise his head to look at the followers, all careful, as ever, not to meet his eye.

As it happened, they were all present, all twelve of them. At these early morning assemblies the procedure was always the same, whether twelve were present or only two or three were gathered together. First, the Skymaster would greet each bird by name. Then he would ask, were all well, had anyone a particular worry or trouble, did anyone need advice? Lastly, all took part in a general chat, where news was exchanged and opinions voiced.

On this particular morning there was of course a good deal of talk about the storm. A number of trees had been blown down in the recent gales, and now all noticed the huge split in the armpit of the Skymaster's branch.

'Good job you weren't sitting there last night, Master,' said Eustace. 'You'd have been...', and then he checked himself on the point of saying 'fried'. The others stared disapprovingly at the little owl, whose mode of address was often, they felt, less than respectful.

Had they been able to look directly into the Skymaster's eyes, they would have seen amusement twinkling there. 'We all have to die some time, Eustace,' he said.

'Not you, Master, surely?' said Loftus.

'We could not do without you,' said Darcy.

'No, no, no!' mewed the buzzards.

'Who would guide us?' asked the kestrel.

'Who would comfort us?' asked the sparrowhawk.

'Who would strengthen us?' asked the hobby.

'You must be with us always,' said Jeb.

'You must watch over us always,' said Myles.

'You will never leave us, Master,' said Glyde.

'Never, Glyde?' said the Skymaster quietly. 'Is this great tree in which we are gathered never to fall? And this branch on which I sit – is it never to break? For it will, my friends. You will see.'

## CHAPTER EIGHT

As well as rabbits and squirrels, many small mammals in Godhanger suffered through the gamekeeper's madness. Stoats and weasels, and even the voles and mice they hunted, crossed the man's path at their peril.

Of the larger animals only the badgers were safe, deep in their sett, and Baldwin was not displeased to find that his lodgers had left. 'Good riddance to bad rubbish,' he grunted.

He had not cared for the smell of them and they were not clean in their habits as were his own kind, who regularly used special latrines a little way away from their holes, and would, at the start of spring, drag out all the old lining from their sleeping-quarters and replace it with fresh bedding of grass and ferns. As for what might have happened to the foxes he neither knew nor cared.

After the death of Flem, Fitz had in fact

stayed on alone in the earth on the fringe of the sett but he was not comfortable there. His bond with his brother had been strong, and for a while he mourned, listless, until the memory began to fade.

Then, one night early in the new year, he was hunting some way from Godhanger when he heard, in a distant copse, the eldritch scream of a vixen seeking a mate. Fitz was a cub no longer but a grown dog-fox almost a year old, and his yapping bark rang out in answer to that alluring invitation. Over the hill he went, never to return to Godhanger again.

As for the roe deer doe, she too left the wood. The constant noise of shooting gave her no rest, and above all she feared for the safety of her two fawns, one male, one female. The night came when, with them following closely behind her, she picked her dainty way down the bed of the stream in which the buck had died. On along its course the three deer went, gradually moving further and further from the place of terror, until at last they found a safe haven, where they could no longer hear the sound of gunfire. Here the doe was one day joined by a handsome buck, his new horns half grown after the autumn shedding of the old ones. Unlike the foxes, the roe had no desire to mate at this season of the year, but now the doe had companionship again, and peace of mind.

Peace of mind was something that Baldwin the badger expected as a right. Heavy and powerful, strong-jawed and sharp-clawed, he feared no animal in the wood but the man and, being a beast of the darkness, did not expect to have truck with him.

So it was with surprise that one night much later, towards the end of the winter, rolling comfortably home with his belly full of worms and snails and beetles and, for good measure, a fat mole that he had dug out of its fortress, Baldwin suddenly smelled man-scent.

What was the killer doing out here, in the middle of the wood, in the pitch darkness, dawn still an hour or more away? Baldwin did not stop to find out but shuffled hastily off to the safety of his sett.

Ever since the burning of the henhouse, the gamekeeper had scoured the wood by day, every day, in search of the one creature he so desperately wanted to kill, but without success. On occasion he had seen the great bird, floating high above, circling endlessly on broad unmoving wings, sometimes in company with a solitary raven, but in the wood, never. By now his marksmanship was almost as of old, so accustomed had he become to the new method he must use, and his injured trigger finger, though still useless, no longer pained him. But of what avail was his skill if the creature never came within range? Nor will it ever, he thought, as long as every damned bird in Godhanger follows me about crying a warning. The jay starts screeching the moment I open the door of my house, and then, wherever I go, they're after me. Blackbirds in every bush cackling at me, magpies, jackdaws and crows somewhere in the trees, there's even a little owl that's got the cheek to join in.

I can't move a step in daylight without being seen, the gamekeeper said to himself, and then, in a flash, he thought – but I could at night! Why didn't I think of it before? It's simple. I get up early, while there's still an hour or so of darkness left and the jay and the rest of them are sleeping, and I find a place to hide where no bird can see me, and I wait, in ambush. When it gets light, I'll be there, waiting, ready, seeing without being seen. With luck, I may find where that blasted thing spends the night. And if I do, it'll be his last! An ambush, that's the way to do it!

But as if on purpose to forestall him, the weather changed for the worse, as though the winter was determined on a last fling before allowing spring upon the stage. For two weeks and more, cold winds blew and cold rains fell night after night, and the gamekeeper could not force himself to leave his warm bed.

Then at last the winds fell light and the sun shone once more, with a hint of warmth in it and a half-promise that the season of rebirth and renewal had begun.

On the following morning, the gamekeeper was already hidden in the depths of the wood, long before the birds of Godhanger began their dawn chorus. He had left his dog chained in her kennel, and, on his way up the garden, had picked up a handful of the ashes of the old hen-house, made porridgy now by the past rains, and rubbed the grey mixture over face and hands. Dark-clothed, his dark shapeless hat pulled down, black-barrelled gun in hand, he made his silent unobserved way to the spot that he had chosen.

It was not in the thickest part of the wood, where he would have had no field of fire if his quarry should appear, but in a small clearing, with a view of a patch of sky overhead. At one side stood a big old oak tree (the very tree, as it happened, that had been home to Gilbert the wild cat). Its massive trunk had been split, perhaps by an ancient lightning-strike, leaving within it a perfect hiding-place in which a tall thin man might conceal himself.

Here, in the darkness, the gamekeeper stood waiting.

Opposite him, across the little clearing, was an ash tree, in the bole of which he could see later as the light strengthened, there was a round knot-hole. As he watched, a figure appeared in the mouth of the hole, the figure of a little owl. Slowly, silently, the gamekeeper raised his gun and took aim. Then he lowered it again, for he knew he must not give away his position for so paltry a prize, and Eustace, all unaware of danger, flew off to the morning meeting.

Of all the followers, Eustace was perhaps the most vulnerable. Glyde, bird solely of the night, was protected by it. Darcy, Myles and Jeb had native cunning and constant alertness on their side. The buzzards and the kestrel spent much of their time hanging at their pitches, high out of harm's way, and the sparrowhawk and the hobby relied on their speed. As for Loftus, he was no woodland bird. Only because of the Skymaster did he ever tear himself away from his sea-cliffs, and always on his visits he conducted himself with the caution and wisdom of great age.

But Eustace, the Skymaster well knew, was most at risk. Bird of both day and night, he was not the greatest of fliers, and in character something of a rebel. In contrast to Glyde's seriousness of manner or Loftus' wariness, Eustace's approach was flippant and devil-may-care.

That morning there were only four at the assembly: the tawny owl, the magpie, the crow and Eustace, and at the end the Skymaster asked the little owl to remain behind for a moment.

'What's up, Master?' said Eustace in his usual pert, almost cheeky way.

'I believe,' said the Skymaster heavily, 'that there is a special danger abroad in Godhanger this day. Danger for you, Eustace. I want you to take great care. Will you give me your word on this?'

'You know best, I'm sure, Master,' said Eustace, 'but everything's as quiet as can be. The jay hasn't screeched, there are no alarm-calls anywhere. I reckon the man's having a nice lie-in.'

'Give me your word,' said the Skymaster again, 'that you will fly straight to that hole of yours in the ash tree, not stopping anywhere for anything, but going directly to safety.'

'Oh, all right,' said Eustace. What's all the fuss about? he thought.

'You promise?'

'I promise, Master.'

Sitting on the storm-torn bough of the cedar, the Skymaster gazed for a long moment upon the little owl. Then he dropped his proud head in a gesture, it seemed, of resignation.

'Go now,' he said quietly, and Eustace flitted away.

He flew straight home in the bright morning light, intending to honour his word, but as he came to the little clearing beside which the ash tree stood, he saw a sudden movement. So still had the gamekeeper stood within the embrace of the old oak's trunk that a woodmouse, in a series of jerky darts, was making a tour of the grass in search of acorns. Forgetting all about his promise, Eustace dropped upon it.

Stiff, tired of waiting, disappointed that his ambush had produced no results, no sign of his quarry, of any quarry, the gamekeeper was not disposed to show mercy twice within the hour.

Out from the oak the black barrels came poking.

★ ★ ★

At that instant there sounded a sudden noise like a mighty rushing wind, and a dark shape came swooping low across the clearing and landed beside Eustace.

Turning to face the gamekeeper, the Skymaster spread his great wings wide over the little owl and his prey, and threw back his head and stared without fear into the twin mouths of the gun.

At the crash of the first shot, Eustace felt the body that covered him slump, so that for a moment one wing pinned him to the ground.

Struggling to free himself, he heard the Skymaster speak in a voice that was strained yet very clear, with a little pause between each word. 'I . . . forgive . . . you.'

Then the gamekeeper stepped out of the oak and fired the second barrel. The body of the Skymaster gave one great convulsive jerk and was still. Released now, Eustace flew madly off, while the woodmouse crawled dazedly away through the bloodstained grasses.

There were many eyes in Godhanger that saw the gamekeeper coming back, holding his victim by the legs, the proud head dragging along the ground, and, later, there was one sharp pair that observed the last rites. The kestrel, hovering high above, saw the man at work by the gibbet.

First he cut down and threw aside the dried-up corpses that already hung upon it, including what was left of the fox. Then he took his latest and greatest quarry and nailed the body to the crosspiece by its wings.

There it hung spread-eagled, the eyes closed, the head hanging upon the breast so that the kestrel could clearly see the golden feathering on the nape of the neck.

'Kee-kee-kee!' called the little falcon harshly, and flew away over the wood.

The gamekeeper stood for a while before the gibbet, staring. He was smiling. He pulled a handful of feathers from the nape and let them fall in a shower of gold. Then he tugged from one wing the biggest of the primary feathers, a long bronze quill that could only have belonged to one bird. Slowly he drew it through his ash-covered fingers before dropping it on the ground. Then he walked down his garden, unchained his dog, and went indoors to clean his gun and make himself some breakfast.

As he sat eating, he heard the wind getting up outside and knew that the weather was on the change again. A gale was blowing up from the west, one of those many gales that had bent and stunted the trees which grew along the hog-mane of Godhanger's horsehead.

Meanwhile in the walnut tree that stood between midden and gibbet, many birds were gathering, birds of all shapes and colours and sizes. There were robins and wrens and tree creepers, chaffinches, bullfinches and goldfinches, blackbirds, thrushes, woodpeckers and many more. The hen jay was there, silent for once as indeed they all were, and so were eleven of the twelve followers, the solitary nightbird, Glyde, having been roused from his sleeping place. Only Loftus, the raven of the sea-cliffs, had not heard the news that the Skymaster had laid down his life for a friend.

For a while, the branches of the walnut, flowering already in early spring though its leaf-buds had not yet burst, were loaded with this silent audience, that sat, swaying in the rising wind, and gazing upon the figure on the gibbet. Then came the sound of an opening door and a dog's bark, and all flew away.

The gamekeeper was setting off for a walk through Godhanger Wood, a walk which was really a triumphal progress. That bloody bird was dead at last, dead as a doornail. It would never trouble him again. He would make the rounds of the wood knowing that it was all his once more.

First he went to the gibbet and looked again upon the shape that hung there, while the spaniel bitch stood up on her hind legs and sniffed at the taloned yellow feet.

Then he began a tour of the wood, while above him the branches of the trees creaked and groaned as the gale strengthened. For once, he could hear no alarm-calls pursuing him, and in fact he saw not a single bird as he went. He returned to the little clearing flanked by the oak and the ash, to savour again this morning's triumph. Then he walked by the stream, to look into the pool in whose depths his rifle lay. Lastly, he went to the edge of the grove, to stand by the cypress tree where first he had glimpsed that damned bird, and fired at it, and winged it, he felt sure.

As the gamekeeper stood there, watching the tossings and swayings of all the huge dark trees of the grove, a feeling came over him that he was no longer in awe of this place, that this morning's death had somehow removed the mystery of it and made it simply another part of his wood.

He walked on into the centre of it, and stood beneath the greatest tree in the grove, a mighty cedar of Lebanon, whose long outstretched arms rose and fell above him as the gale swept through. One large bough, he noticed, had somehow split half away from the trunk, and he paused beneath it, squinting upwards to assess the damage. As he stood there, thinking that he would return when the weather was calmer and cut it off, for it would provide many sweet-smelling logs for his cottage fire, his dog began to whine. Then suddenly it dashed away, still whimpering. He called it, shouting above the howl of the wind, but his voice was drowned by a sudden loud, cracking, tearing noise, as the wounded branch of the cedar of Lebanon, the branch upon which the Skymaster had always sat, fell with a shattering crash upon the gamekeeper and crushed the life out of him.

Loftus came in from the cliffs that afternoon, hoping to see, as he often did, the Skymaster wheeling high above Godhanger. Because the raven had not attended that morning's gathering, he felt that perhaps he might make some apology for his absence.

The gale carried him across the intervening fields in a matter of minutes but there was no great familiar shape to be seen on high, only a scatter of rooks, spinning like black leaves in the westerly.

Then, at the edge of the wood, he saw the kestrel, perched on a topmost branch. The gale was too strong for the little bird to live up to his other name of 'windhover', and he clung tightly to his wildly swaying perch as the raven dropped down beside him.

'Have you seen the Master today?' Loftus called in his deep tones.

'Yes. Have you not?'

'No, I was not at the gathering.'

'Nor I. But I have seen him since.'

'Where?'

'Hung upon the gibbet. The man shot him. Our Master is dead,' said the kestrel, and, crying his harsh sad cry, he swooped from his perch and was whirled away.

'He cannot be,' said Loftus. 'It cannot be true.' He took off and flew on across the wood.

He went straight to the grove. 'He will be there,' said Loftus. 'He must be there. The kestrel must be wrong.'

But though he croaked loudly, high above the cedar, there was no answer. A great branch had fallen from the tree, Loftus saw, and somewhere a dog was howling.

The raven flew on, and to every bird he saw, he cried, 'Have you seen the Master?' and all replied, 'We have seen him. He is dead. He hangs upon the gibbet.'

At last, as he crossed a small clearing, he saw the little figure of Eustace, standing in the mouth of his ash-tree hole, and he swerved to land upon a lower branch.

'Tell me it is not so, Eustace,' croaked Loftus. 'They say the Master is dead. Tell me it is not so.'

For a while the little owl did not answer. He stood like a small statue and stared, not at the raven, but at the oak tree across the clearing, and at the ruffled patch between, where a few feathers lay among the blood-dappled grasses.

'Well?' said Loftus.

'It was all my doing,' said Eustace.

'You! What can you mean? The man shot him, they all say.'

'So he did,' said Eustace. 'Here, in this clearing, and has come back since, to gloat. But the Master came here to save me. I disobeyed him, and should have paid with my life. But he saved it, at the cost of his own, covering me with his sheltering wings. He deliberately sacrificed himself. He died that I might live. A bad bargain, you might say.'

Loftus looked up at the little owl, usually so

pert and jolly, and saw the grief in his yellow eyes. Then he looked down, and saw the feathers in the dark-stained grass.

Then a sudden shaft of understanding pierced his mind, and he said some very wise things. 'Eustace,' he said. 'You must not blame yourself. He has forgiven you, of that I am sure. He would not want you to be for ever heavy of heart.'

Then Loftus flew away towards the eye of the horsehead until he saw below, at the top of the gamekeeper's garden, the midden by the broken pigsty wall, and the walnut tree, and beyond it, the gibbet.

There was nothing on it.

The old raven dropped down into the tree and looked carefully at the T-shaped wooden structure, and saw, at its foot, a scatter of golden feathers and one long bronze quill that could only have belonged to one bird.

The Master had been there then, had hung there as they said, but he was no longer there. Had the man taken him down from the gibbet, then? He must have done.

Loftus sat for a long time in the walnut, its branches quiet again for the gale had blown itself out, and the evening sky showed promise of a better day to come. As well as his grief for the death of the Skymaster he felt a special small sadness, remembering something that the Master had once said to him.

'Your eyes, my friend,' he had said, 'shall be the last to see me.' But that had not come to pass.

Wearily, the raven flew away towards the changeless sea.

The trees of Godhanger were still and quiet again as Baldwin left the badgers' sett to begin his night's foraging. The noise of the storm had not bothered him as he lay curled snugly in his well-lined bed-chamber, any more than the constant sound of gunfire that had filled so many days. Baldwin took no notice of such things. The centre of his world was the great sett, where badgers had lived long before men with guns, long before men with bows and arrows, long even before men with stone-axes. The day was for sleep, the night for hunting, and though Baldwin was fiercely loyal to the family of which he was the head, his principal loyalty was to his belly. Now it felt very empty, and he trotted along through the wood, stopping now and again to pick up something edible or to roll or to give himself a good scratching.

His route that night took him towards the grove. For Baldwin, this strange place held no terrors. He was afraid of nothing, save for the man. Now as he made his way over the mossy floor beneath the foreign evergreens, there came to his questing nose that feared scent, and he stopped in his tracks, ready for instant retreat and flight.

His eyes saw no movement, his ears heard none, but his nose told him clearly that the man was near. Yet the scent was subtly different. Instinct told him that somehow the man was no longer a threat, and his nosiness drew him nearer, towards the fallen cedar branch.

In the fitful light of the moon the badger could now see that there was something sticking out from under the dark broken bough. It was a hand, that had once been a strong right hand. Now not merely one, but all its fingers were useless.

His curiosity satisfied, Baldwin shuffled away across the grove, grunting unconcernedly, his mind on more important things.

When Loftus left him, Eustace had shuffled backwards into the darkness of his ash-tree home. He had had enough of staring out into the clearing, replaying the death scene in his mind. If only that damned mouse hadn't been running about there, he thought. If only I had resisted the temptation to drop on it. If only . . .

Exhausted by the horror of the day, Eustace fell into a sleep that was at first dreamless. But then a picture began to form in his mind, as he slept, a picture of a great familiar shape, not broken and bloody and shot-torn, but whole and hale and in perfect plumage. And the Skymaster spoke clearly to him, saying, 'Blame not yourself, little owl Eustace. And mourn not for me, for all is well that has ended well, as my life has. Yours is still before you, to be enjoyed as befits your happy nature, not to be wasted in regret. Live it to the full, Eustace, for my sake.'

Eustace woke from his dream with a start. From being the picture of gloom, he suddenly felt excited and filled with energy; glad to be alive. He clicked his beak and bowed his head rapidly up and down as he peered out of the hole in the ash.

In a few moments another woodmouse appeared, to scuttle about in the grass below.

Or perhaps you're the same one as before, said Eustace to himself. Either way, you're a damned mouse. And he launched himself upon it.

* * *

Crouched beside his mate on their ledge under the cliff top, Loftus spent much of a restless night thinking about his dead Master and of what an extraordinary being he was. What he had meant to the others, thought Loftus, I shall never know, but now he has laid down his life for one of theirs. To me he was above all a friend. However long I live (and surely at my age that cannot be much longer) I shall never forget him.

Towards dawn Loftus dozed uneasily a while, and then, as the light grew stronger, the hen raven stretched herself, and drew her massive black bill across the shaggy feathers of his throat in a gesture of long affection.

'Shall we hunt?' she said.

'You go,' Loftus said. 'I am a little tired this morning. I shall rest a while longer.'

When his mate had gone, Loftus sat for a time, staring down at the sea far below, a sea calm now after the passing of the gale. Then he hopped off his ledge, let the updraught take him, and pitched down again on the short sheep-nibbled turf of the cliff top.

Behind him, to the east, the sun came up over the hog-mane of Godhanger and lit up a stipple of little fine-weather clouds high in the blue of the sky. The season of rebirth was in the air.

As he turned towards the warmth of the sun, the old raven suddenly fancied that he could see a distant figure rise out of Godhanger. He poked his head forward, trying to make out – for his eyesight seemed somehow to have dimmed – what sort of bird it was.

Then the figure began to fly westwards towards him, with slow majestic wing-beats, and as it neared him, Loftus, head thrown back now to stare upwards, saw beyond any shadow of a doubt that it was the Skymaster, who had surely died, yet even now was rising up into the morning sky.

Loftus opened his bill, but no words came from it, only a hoarse croak as he gazed up towards this vision high overhead.

Round and round it swung in wide circles, climbing, climbing all the while, growing smaller and smaller, until at last it vanished into a great cloud that had appeared, a cloud strangely shaped, like a giant bird with mighty wings outspread.

Loftus' head fell forward on his breast.

In Godhanger Wood there was birdsong everywhere, heralding the birth of new life, new hope.

Everywhere the trees had begun to burst out

into leaf, and in one of them sat a visitor to the wood, freshly arrived.

'Cuckoo!' he called. 'Cuckoo! The spring is here!'

## THE END